The King of the Storeroom

Antonio Porta

The King of the Storeroom

Lawrence R. Smith, translator

WESLEYAN UNIVERSITY PRESS

Published by University Press of New England

Hanover and London

WESLEYAN UNIVERSITY PRESS
Published by University Press of New England,
Hanover, NH 03755

This translation copyright © 1992 by Lawrence R. Smith;
originally published in 1978 as *Il re del magazzino* by
Arnoldo Mondadori Editore, Milan, Italy, © Antonio Porta.
Rights granted by the heirs of Antonio Porta.

All rights reserved

Printed in the United States of America   5 4 3 2 1
CIP data appear at the end of the book

Contents

Translator's Note 7

Preliminary Remarks 9

DAY ONE 11

DAY TWO 15

DAY THREE 17

DAY FOUR 19

DAY FIVE 23

DAY SIX 29

DAY SEVEN 31

DAY EIGHT 37

DAY NINE 41

DAY TEN 45

DAY ELEVEN 51

DAY TWELVE 55

DAY THIRTEEN 61

DAY FOURTEEN 65

DAY FIFTEEN 73

DAY SIXTEEN 77

DAY SEVENTEEN 83

DAY EIGHTEEN 93

DAY NINETEEN 97

DAY TWENTY 101

DAY TWENTY-ONE 105

DAY TWENTY-TWO 107

No Number 111

DAY TWENTY-THREE 115

DAY TWENTY-SIX 123

DAY TWENTY-SEVEN 127

DAY TWENTY-EIGHT 131

DAY TWENTY-NINE 137

DAY THIRTY-ONE 141

DAY THIRTY-TWO 147

Translator's Note

My special thanks go to John Picchione, Professor of Italian at York University in Toronto, for his crucial assistance. He read over this manuscript, pointed out errors, and gave me many helpful suggestions. I would also like to thank Eastern Michigan University for awarding me a one year research fellowship, during which I completed this translation.

November 1991   L.R.S.

Preliminary Remarks

I found this handwritten manuscript in a little storage room (a kind of basement, maybe it was once an actual cellar for food and wine) almost buried under the rubble of a Lombard farmhouse destroyed by the recent rains and earthquake jolts. Yes, I can assure you I really found it there. When I opened the cardboard tub to see if there was any laundry detergent (as the label declared) I found instead sheets of paper scrolled up inside. The container was right next to a sitting man, sitting but folded over on top of his legs, having apparently died in that position, a puppet with slack strings. He was in a pretty good state of preservation and looked just as I would (and many others like me) if I were in that position, sitting and then folded over on myself. I closed up the storeroom, reconstructed the rubble grave, and got right to work transcribing. It was almost like performing my own funeral rites. Now I know saying this will immediately start little waves of queasiness and antibodies of repulsion running through you. But that's the way it is, and the way it's got to be, for me and maybe for the others as well. I've finished a complete transcription with the care and precision of a philologist, in homage to the old masters. Yet I still don't know how much good my life crossing his will do me; the future will tell. Anyway, there's a little line of his I like to say to myself, and it helps: I'll make everything new.

Day One

I watch the crystal clear water flowing by. The riverbanks are covered with new grass. Willows, acacias, and other Po Valley trees, like the leafy poplars, see their trembling leaves mirrored on the water's surface. A slow early-summer breeze moves across the plain. As I sit here writing these lines, notebook on my lap, Bic pen between my fingers, I look at the crystal clear water. I'm sure I won't be parched much longer; my thirst will finally be quenched. Thanks to the crystal purity of these waters which gurgle like my throat. I'm very thirsty, and that's made even worse by the wear and tear I've gone through to get to the peaceful Lambro on foot. It is the river of my childhood, when its waters were as clear as they are now, and I'd lie down on the bank plunging first my tongue, then my face, and finally my entire head into the water.

Then the use of the adjectives "crystal" and "clear" for the noun "water" seemed redundant, an Arcadian frill. Those words had more to do with painting than nature, more to do with frescoes where that genre of poetry continued long after the disappearance of fake shepherds. When some people gifted with *bon sens* warned that it wasn't so much a question of protecting "landscapes" as it was not getting in the way of life, many decided it was best to take problems on a case by case basis *in order to* or *in view of* (such quick action!) and the course of the Lambro River, in spite of declarations which appeared daily in the "press," was turned into that mush called "liquid waste." Those who had warned against getting in the way of life weren't aware they were going against the course of History (by that I mean the History of Capitalism, naturally), and at the same time the use of the adjectives "crystal" and "clear" became indispensible when referring to the water, which was really more like "shitty."

If the river had not turned back into water I would have died of thirst by now. None of the fountains work anymore, at least none of the ones I found on my way here, and not even the ones I discovered in the almost deserted city. An irreparable breakdown must have first blocked and subsequently destroyed, over a period of a few months, the entire water network: the Lombard aqueduct, maybe the whole Italian aqueduct as well. The wreckage couldn't be seen because it was all underground, and the pumps were hidden in old Sforza-style fortified towers which had since been reduced to heaps of ancient bricks. The surviving hydraulics experts, and for a time there were some, couldn't do anything about it because they couldn't find the network's Masterplan, the so-called "Water Map." It was locked up in municipal buildings inside old, medieval-looking wooden cabinets, and they had been turned to ashes by one of the innumerable fires that suddenly flared up all over the place, near and far (Vigevano City Hall and a Sanctuary in Piedmont, for example). The people said it was like magic, as if giant matches had been scratched into flame on the rough asphalt streets. Needless to say, those matches were just the regular kind (safety or book matches) we don't have anymore, since the last ones were used enjoying those bonfires. Overcome by despair, the last arsonists threw themselves into the flames and finished a spectacle that didn't even have the power to make us shudder anymore. Fewer and fewer spectators watched, but this was also due to the exodus and the fact that people were simply disappearing.

Before finishing up writing for today (and so you're finally going to take your drink, says someone intolerant of Rhetorical Devices) I want to make a note (and I certainly will) of how much I enjoy writing by hand again. By that I mean without hitting typewriter keys, which had become an obsession for me, especially at the end. In order to survive I had to take part in the Universal Conversation Without Reply, thus abusing the instrument as well as my handwriting (clear or hard to read as it may be), to say nothing of my intellect being reduced to shreds. It has just occurred to me that the sound or noise of the keyboard was building a cage around my head (like the ones the Chinese use for crickets), and it kept tightening until I had to stop typing, because nothing was left inside the red-hot cage; the cricket lay there squashed and couldn't even remember what he was doing. To get back to normal he had to leave the house without delay and walk rapidly for at least an hour through either city or countryside, it didn't matter which.

Day Two

Having made the transition from idyll to necessity (when the river was "liquid waste," you moved instead from necessity to idyll and the fake farmers, fake shepherds, fake wild men, etc. multiplied throughout the countryside, within the ecological mirage), having quenched my thirst, I plunged my entire head into the water so the coolness could go all the way to the roots of my hair and after that down to my innards. Therefore, I have suspended my writing.

I once saw a movie where the protagonist was sentenced to life in prison. He kept his mind alive with a series of exercises for his imagination. As the first exercise he decided to recall all the evenings he had ever spent at the opera, and he managed to make both words and music sing again, from first note to last. Then he got involved in complex calculations without the use of either pencil or paper; he was able to project symbols and numbers on the wall as if he had put up a sheet for a movie. Then he pretended he had a class before him and he was teaching it, chalk in hand. For his muscles he set up a series of indoor calisthenic exercises a fanatical father had taught him and he had hated. Now they kept him from rotting.

And the same thing with the exercise we call writing. I'm sure of this: as long as I can get my hands on notebooks or paper of any kind, I won't stop. After that I'll write on an imaginary movie screen sheet. I don't want to end up like all the ones I meet who are no longer capable of words, having short-circuited, as they say, the symbolic system of our species and being forced to use violent gestures and barks, which negate the desire to communicate implicit even in howling. It goes without saying that I'll also have to find something to eat. I plan to read my writings to people like me and ask for a potato in return, or a turnip, not just bitter roots.

I believe the desire (necessity?) to hear speech, to talk and listen, even to the sound of simple phrases we often say just to make an echo, has not disappeared. As for now I know about a storeroom off by itself, partially buried, and it's given me a good source of supplies, which I plan to build up as soon as possible and use as little as possible.

Day Three

I have another way of using my hands. I belong to that class of men who can do almost nothing with their hands, except use certain tools created by ancient technology. I knew how to make a "beautiful" cup of coffee, as the Neapolitans say, but without gas I haven't yet found a way to see if I still remember how. I don't know how to make even the most elementary tools: the best I could do was sharpen a spoon handle for digging up good roots, ones that aren't too bitter. Writing is the only way to put my hands to good use, and I've got to depend on it. So I'm going to tell my potential audience a little of what has happened (or at least what I've understood of what has happened) as if it were a fable, just as I would write a story, building it up piece by piece to help understand things better, or rather to understand them at all. This is the purpose it serves and will continue to serve. If you have an attic or cellar, you always keep things you should throw away. After some years or perhaps some decades, everything turns out to be useful again and regains market value, at times a very high price on the market, like the imitations that become hot items for the antique trade. There is even a world market for them (enough to make you choke, in this case). I'm putting the least cumbersome thing possible (or so it appears) in my little storeroom of food supplies: the burden of memory transformed into story. It's up to others to say if it's worth anything, if my labor is productive.

I'll also write a little about what is happening, happening to me right now, and I'm afraid this might be the most monotonous part, a listing of facts that shouldn't be very surprising. And yet you never know. As I said before, you've got to really get into something before you can know anything about it. Right now I'd rather relax in the shade of a bush. They used to call it an "umbrella." A tree in the middle of a field that farmers sat under when they wanted to stop and catch their breath. Or travelers. This winter is never going to be over; it's so hot it's going to end up setting everything on fire. There are boxes of unbroken crackers in the storeroom and I've gorged them all down. To hell with wild roots. With this humidity I've got to lie down and take a rest or I'll explode. Burps and farts are saving my life.

Day Four

I heard it on the radio one morning, a little before eight (solar time). They were discussing and debating the rate of inflation, which they called the "creeping plague" and diagnosed as a "slow poisoning" of an economy that would eventually end up stone dead. That was all quite true, in and of itself, but you also knew some people profited from inflation. The rich became richer, at least in the "short run," and then in the "long run" too, because they took over the land—fields and hills alike. They followed the myopic but unbeatable scheme (the ones who tried to beat it ended up losing) of good, old-fashioned speculation. So you had the suspicion, you might almost say the certainty, of being tricked even by those analyses which seemed beyond reproach, precise economic science. But if someone came to tell us that "two and two equals four," as Don Giovanni got it straight from the mouth of Leporello, we ended up thinking "five." The rest (to be understood, "of the damage") kept up their endless talk and phony debating, most of which was cosmeticized so that, by burying itself under an unbroken fabric of cleverly linked words, it mixed truth and lies *ad infinitum*, reducing our picture of the world, and of labor relations in particular, to mush. You read that the movement was crushing the opportunists: unfortunately, later (too late, as is always the case) we found out that they had actually enlarged the holes in the tearing social fabric.

With this intellectual mush something analogous to the tale of Little Red Riding Hood took place. You know, the story Perrault wrote with an *unhappy* ending: Little Red Riding Hood died in the wolf's belly and that was it. Immediately or almost immediately after that was written, the Germans of all people invented a good hunter (but the Germans think hunters are always "good," otherwise they're not real hunters) who kills the wolf, opens his belly and pulls the child out alive. No, Perrault insists, she turned into wolf shit. No, you can get along with inflation, say the others, the hunters.

A German journalist, who was living very happily "down in the sun" in Italy, was dragged into a radio debate at this time. He reminded them that in the time of the Great Inflation (1922) the process of dissolution became so rapid the workers had to be paid twice a day to survive. At this point an ingenious government minister invented the "agricultural mark"; Germany was saved and the Nazis began to prepare for their takeover. "Agricultural mark" meant that you anchored the value of paper money to products of the earth (crops). Suddenly the farmers were rich. Germany was powerful again and was driven to a thirst for even more by this superior new philosophy, which had been quickly obtained by making a few small manipulations of "ordinary" philosophy. But people didn't make these connections then. An indelible photo has remained printed (literally) on my mind: the image of wheelbarrows full of paper money needed to buy a kilogram of bread. Again and again, every time I tallied up my daily expenses, the image of the wheelbarrows leaped forward in my mind. You can get along without a car, and I got along without one, but bread at ten thousand lira had to have been the beginning of the last phase of the catastrophe. We know it was. The day after: twenty thousand. At four that afternoon: thirty thousand. Union disputes were declared "open" or "perpetual," as in the revolution of utopian memory. Exactly at midnight the vampires announced new wages calculated by 24 hour periods, then every twelve hours, beginning with the campanile bells at noon.

So that was the way a 15 minute morning radio broadcast became (as I look back now) one of the Useless Signals chance or necessity put right in front of our eyes. But we all looked on passively, without deciphering the ultimate consequences; that's the way we spent the time that stood between us and the Black Hole. But to go on living (the certainty of the final consequences wasn't apparent to us then), we needed those microscopic doses of hope that made us believe in the optimistic version of the black fairy tale. Yet hope, which we were sure we couldn't do without (and that's a mistake, a crazy idea that got stamped into the brain of our species), is alcohol, drugs, poison.

When the Minister of the Economy, the seventeenth in just a few months (he wanted to be called the eighteenth, because of an astrological superstition he increasingly emphasized, leading someone to remark: "fortune tellers directly to power!" and I refused to answer the usual question "what's your sign?"), who had heard the same radio program I did, decided to "introduce the agricultural lira," there were no more potatoes, turnips, or bags of corn to use as an anchor. The Great Warehouses, emptied by the same people who had filled them, would burn in a matter of a few hours, two or three days at most. That was when they came up with the idea of setting everything on fire (with the "final matches," we said jokingly, and we laughed until it hurt, because we knew that *in reality* these would actually be the last ones). Doesn't it make you laugh even now? Right after that someone blew the whistle, on the radio as always, saying that part (or all?) of the Lombard agricultural reserves had been used to resupply nuclear bomb shelters in Switzerland. Reaction: indifference, as if no one had said a thing. Recovery was impossible.

Ate two turnips and a red apple. Drank red wine from the storeroom. The last bottle of Teroldego. Some of you might be curious to know why I'm adding these notes on such everyday matters. They work like a calendar.

Day Five

Early this morning a small stroke of luck that has increased the probability I'll be able to write longer than I had anticipated. You know, it's more than a problem of finding paper and ink. The act of writing is a kind of labor too, so I need projects and programs.

The lucky find was sheets of poetry—both loose sheets and a notebook—that I wrote for my children in the form of letters, but didn't mail. They left me slowly, with precise rips at the various stages of growing up: childhood, adolescence, and finally adulthood. That was when they started trying to get back in touch again and I thought I'd answer them with these letters. Now I have a chance to rewrite them at my leisure, so I can really understand them thoroughly—as I was always at great pains to do. Then I'll be able to collect them into a packet, put them in a clear plastic bag, hang it from a branch, and wait for someone to come along. A passerby can take the bag and start the letters on their final journey. It's a new kind of postal system: casual, full of suspense. You can stand there and watch for the first pick-up, and then follow him and see if there's a second, and so on.

But I can also read them in the evenings I've imagined for myself: the desire to listen, to re-establish the sequence of events, the need for narration, for ordered, rhythmical communication. They will help me reconstruct and re-establish the calendar of the past year, which otherwise seems to have been totally destroyed by those last flames. And which I will now in part reconstruct by other means (the story).

The title I gave to these poems was: Short Letters to Two Children. And naturally I'm going to keep it.

Letter No. 1

(I) ask myself, should I go to the window
to see Mr. B.B. in his Chinese jacket, without glasses
take that little morning stroll around his house
(I) stand there watching and tell myself it's so simple,
it's so simple; my son and daughter need to
    understand,
understand and not give themselves up for dead before
    they even go away
I walk into my son's and daughter's house with a cat
    in my arms
so they'll keep me in their laps, even when I'm gone,
    like a cat
we're looking out the window, waiting for B.B. to
    appear
with half-closed eyes and I'll be able to say: keep your
    eyes open
and the cat will give us a signal

3/25/76

Letter No. 2

(I) ask you to touch me here on my back and sides
if I open my legs which they've stuck full of pins
starving pink mice run around the delicate pubic skin
there were about six banderillas, they worked me over
    pretty well
the others always on horseback (I) on foot, a sack of
    beans on my back
this is work I'm talking about and I get up when I'm
    through
I do two or three knee bends and you watch me,
    laughing
you must know I need to do them but in reverse

3/28/76

Letter No. 3

(I) stand on a little stepladder to see
what my scrotum looks like between the asshole and
    prick
they've shaved everything off between cock and
    sphincter
if I tell you a thousand hands have stroked me
that I can't tell one from another anymore
that I feel like a smooth, flat surface
like your adolescent peach-fuzz cheek, without worms
if I do the can-can I feel a tingling sensation
standing on the stairs I eat grapes, balls, I do bowel
    movements
I sit on the toilet and seem to be shitting out little
vampires: make sure you don't believe me when I tell
    you what I'm doing
as if: but open up quickly or I'll tell you I'm speaking
from inside the closet with a clock in my stomach

3/28/76

Day Six

A bit of back page news. There were six bottles of Marzemino and now there are only five. Either I count badly and remember worse (I'm not going to bother over accounts anymore—I promise that any further notes will be more useful than these punctilious ones) or someone else is hiding out in the Lambro area, and following me, but he doesn't have the nerve or the opportunity, or maybe even the need, for a complete burglary job. He'd need his own wheelbarrow and a heavy rope, like the one in *Mother Courage*. He's hoping I'll acknowledge his presence and then let him go on living, at least for the time being. There aren't any guns, and I'm not going to strangle him. That reminds me of just how far away the Great Thieves are, the ones who cleaned out the Warehouses the day before the announcement of the "agricultural lira." We suspected it at the time, but now we're certain it was that same Minister who directed their last movements and made all the big decisions. At the precise moment the self-styled "parties of the left" gave their vote of confidence for the seventeenth time (without asking to share power in a coalition), the Minister made the decisive move which proved him to be the shrewdest and most opportunistic of all the Great Thieves. They deserve the capital letters because they were the ones who created the framework of the Second

Society which vampirized the First. Before the big caper they ran the State (which was supposed to be Advanced Capitalism), the Bureaucracy, and the Class Struggle, just as if the whole thing were true—there in the Grand Theater. Meanwhile, the Dormice operated secretively and undisturbed behind the scenes, gnawing the support beams, which seemed to be intact right up to the last moment. If someone happened to be found out, there was always another Shadow-Dormouse to take his place, and the one who came to light was willingly sacrificed to the public's demand for honesty and integrity. An old smuggler's trick, always leaving something behind for the Customs Officers. And he enjoyed the hoax even after the final act, because it was the ex-Minister himself who told us (in a radio tape of six installments) the whole story from beginning to end, as if it were a fairy tale. The politics of fantasy? Who would dare believe anything else?

Toward evening an airplane very high with gleaming contrails. Watched a long time without hearing the sound of the jet engines. An apparition, since no one can get kerosene. A phantasm projected according to a schedule and a flight path recorded in my memory who knows how long ago. I woke up in the night to the noise of another one landing at Linate, in a darkness as deep as Heaven itself.

Day Seven

I ask myself how I could have seen an airplane at high altitude with a shiny tail yesterday, and with jet engines which couldn't exist (I should have heard the sound). And then there was the other that landed at Linate in darkness (was it flying with no lights?) I only heard. Airplanes like kites. Like weather balloons? Hope? I don't like to fly: it always seems like some new-fangled menace, as if we had not yet touched bottom, and in fact we never will. UFO. Fear. Crystal clear waters of my childhood and certain flowers, impalpable, the fermenting pepper tree, with the sound of airplane engines, different and yet the same as the one that landed last night at Linate. The sky brought thunderstorms and bombs. A bomb is like a statue in the garden; it chases evil spirits away. The statue bites its tail, gets mad, explodes. Goddamned prop planes: I still hear them, and always at night. I love you and I don't love you. No, I don't want you anymore.

Letter No.4

I'm not a stone poet like Beckett
I don't question papier-mâché heavens in the theater
I confess I don't know how to read constellations
looking up and marveling in the courtyard
but I use word-constellations as mosaics, I compose
    and recompose
so we can speak this language these languages
    together
let's lift up language and see what's underneath
let's speak the unveiled word with its shameless roots
(I'm sending you this note for further reference)

4/10/76

From the top of the hill, at the end of the almost perpendicular ascent that leads to Brunate, you could see the city burn at night. There was a large boulevard with a man hanging from every tree; now there are only photographs. This is how they did it: shoot them in the legs, breaking them so they give way and the body slumps to the ground, pulling the noose tight around the neck.

This was my childhood and early adolescence; our nonrepresentative democracy and I grew up together. Sadistic, and I can confidently assert this after thirty years (the capital S stands for structure, as far as I'm concerned). If you say Sadistic and watch from this Tower, you'll discover things you never noticed before.

Letter No. 5

I saw a child on TV, he said
"if the children cried
they shot them if the children
didn't cry they didn't shoot them
they shoved them into the canal
along with the others they shoved they cried
they shoved them into the canal they shot the
    survivors
they burned the ones who ran home
they cut down the banana trees the shacks
they shot the ones who were crying in the canal
and then they went away"
I ask you, does this seem highly rhetorical?

April, no date

Letter No.6

you tell me a story: the cop handcuffed them to an
    iron fence
in the Piazza Stuparich with its gate and Charlie
Mingus—then he whacked him in the balls with a
    night stick and said
does it hurt? the answer was: yes! and then he hit him
again and the answer was: no! then he stopped and the
    rest stopped
doing it to the others who were also handcuffed to the
    gate
now you know I've given you a simple truth
I swear the Nazis and their camps are here among us
they're not here among us just to be nice but they're
setting up so they can relay signals (Pinochet is a man
    of his word)
they can be ready to go in the wink of an eye with
    their well-preserved
original plans along with torture manuals both
    ancient
and modern just like anatomical theaters where
    antique lancets
are polished and hung on the walls for our admiration
    and I'm sending you a big hug

4/13/76

A wonderful turnip with real table salt (I have more: the thief stole two packets and that's all, where's he gone off to now?). A friend taught me this when the times were only moderately calamitous, saying: if something happens the folks around here will all die of hunger and cold. They're just not used to anything. Eat a turnip; nobody knows how good they are. It's a miracle that someone is still growing them: a stubborn old farmer, I guess. So we ate them together and knew we were right to talk about such things, but not even we could believe what we were saying would really come true. Wasn't the miracle of the turnip there to give us hope? But we said: "let's put hay in the barn; if we don't need it now, we sure will sometime later." If I hadn't remembered this I wouldn't have been able to carry off a sack of turnips no one else saw from a store that was suddenly without its owners. (Had they run away, or were they dying of hepatitis somewhere?) Now what can I say: wonderful, one more time. It seems to be the beginning of utopia and its end as well—a necessity, the beginning of another life.

Day Eight

They killed the lights on the airport runway. He says: "We were ready to turn them back on again." He replies: "The nearest airplane was flying over Bologna at the moment, and we knew it." "Why did you turn them out?" "You know exactly why. We work in impossible conditions. Why don't you come and see for yourselves?" "But don't you realize you've gone *too far*, that this goes way beyond any acceptable protest?" "That's not true." "It's as if you wanted to kill someone." "We wanted to divert them, that's all. If a plane had been running short on fuel, we were ready to turn the lights back on." "But no one believes this, because your action can be reduced to a single phrase: *they snuffed them out*, inevitable, twisted, excessive, as we have already stated. Taking this all together, one thing is very clear: the turned off lights stand for catastrophe and death." But everyone kept quiet and no one replied: "You answer death with death."

A life so impossible, you can't understand it anymore. Like migratory birds going north instead of south just before the beginning of winter. It's suicide: confronted by this impulse everything had to come to a halt, between the two contesting parties, I mean. Of course, there was the duplicity of their system of communication: it was impossible to (or you were unable to) tell the actual truth without destroying yourself by seeming to overstate the case, so that it came back on your head with redoubled force in the echo made by the guy who recognized and manipulated your mistake and breathed life into conspiracies of Terror, fleshed out Anxiety into an ugly little creature.

Then the trial and the acquittal: they didn't want to kill, they were prepared *not to do it*. The *as if* was removed, but not erased. And then the dream of armed struggle.

(I sharpened the diver's knife I keep hidden in the picnic basket to make sure the storeroom thief doesn't get it. I'm putting this part of my writings in parentheses to remind myself not to read it to anyone, or else they'll come right over and steal my knife. But I hid it in a new place. I give up. The thief is an old man who crawls around on all fours, on his elbows, legs half rigid, an old man from the operetta with only a few days to live. If it really becomes necessary: no knife, no bloody mess, I'll just crush his head behind the bush where he crouches and hides, where it'll be easy to sneak up on him. He'll hide all by himself, the corpse! My dear mother would always say to me: but how do these crazy ideas get into your head?! We don't know what we might do just to overcome our loneliness—crawl, leap! beyond the boundaries we're forced to live within.... But surely we do know, and it's still true we have the desire to kill, and that we know how to bury this profound vocation with the power to eat ourselves alive. All alone. Self-devourers. This was the reason Laura, a real protagonist in a love novel, and what a love!, agreed to eat a sandwich full of shit, her own. And the clean cut, between the two, made by anal intercourse? Isn't that a stab wound?)

(Parenthesis, like a wall. At certain points I have to draw this sign of separation, but not of separateness: I want to be able to put it in or take it out whenever it seems necessary to do so. And when will it seem necessary? Barbed wire. Glass from broken bottles, a dry wall covered with brambles. . . . When the urge to communicate becomes so strong and pushes on the embankment with such force that the little dike collapses and writing flows out, and manifests itself as work, my work, and is put to use, it must always be useful—that hyperdelicate mechanism, like a hand. . . .)

Day Nine

"The Great Belly of the World needs a laxative."

This was the top line on a poster printed and pasted up by the Friars (ex-Franciscans, Ex-Capuchins, etc.) on walls all over the city. "No spray paint manifestos," they declared in spray paint on church walls, both inside and out. This was the way they demonstrated their decision to re-enter the wall communications competition. But they had lost a lot of ground over the years, especially with the declining popularity of holy pictures (decline, not death).

And right under this poster someone wrote: "This laxative is a ten megaton bomb, ready to go and it'll be used as a suppository." It was easy for the monks, with their Rabelaisian tradition, to get right into this kind of Grotesquery and keep the spirit of the sewer going: "Now degraded humanity will drown in its own shit, expelled by the Explosion."

They ran through the city with their rolled-up posters under their arms, in their shit-colored robes, bare feet filthy with shit, beards down to their chests, heads down, fugitives not pursuers, unpunished, threatened by the barking of chained dogs. They showed us Ignorance was synonymous with Salvation, and also that we should ignore the fact that the apocalyptic crusade they were feeding had hidden supporters who knew enough to stay out of sight, in orbit, ready to descend into the religious void created by the Friars and carry out the Last Judgment. But in the meanwhile, said the malicious (the anti-clerics, viewed with more and more suspicion), the number of donations requested and received grew enormously, and the surplus, after maintenance and living expenses, was reinvested in the Crusade.

There was always a growing number of people, continually belabored by the bombardments of this phony, tyrannical religion, who would rather have their eyes squirt out of their sockets than stoop to cutting deals with the enemy. So the fascination with the Apocalypse grew in these longing souls, and ever more clearly the vision of the Great Explosion entered into their wishful dreams. They thought the Mushroom would put a hole in the Van Allen belts, and from that hole the rain of celestial purification would fall and wipe out Sin forever.

Minorite paranoia was apparently limited to the followers of the Friars, so the danger of an epidemic was underestimated—even when the President was elected, the one who was supposed to be so religious, who stopped wherever he was and prayed ten times a day: playing tennis, in his swimming pool or helicopter, and other times had the violent and often embarrassing impulse to fuck, which was immediately (or almost immediately) repressed, resulting in the swellings that appeared all over his body, and that later led to flaccid tumors.

But the tendency to underestimate this possible danger came from the belief that if the religious madness really were the prevailing force, it would be apparent to all. There would be no holding back the heavy but impalpable landslide pushing against the citadel of reason. Not enough of us realized that the citadel had already been abandoned by many of its former inhabitants. They had been infected by that rhetorical murmur, overwhelmed by mysterious desires which needed only a little internal twisting to find a religious outlet.

(Weren't the Friars reading the Scriptures during their silent meals? I wouldn't be able to do as much living in a small community, granted that I found one and they took me in, even for just two potatoes cooked under the coals. One day to insult me they called out "professor!" And I answered: "no, sorry, I'd like to but I can't." They thought I'd given them a lunatic's response, that I had nothing to teach. What I knew, and I still know a little bit, I got like everyone else from under the infinite layers of mystification, which opened up for only a few brief moments and then that unbearable weight slid back into place. It became the world again, and covered up the works of man with its funereal pall.

Now I have nothing really important for my hands to do, and the work is to be done by my hands alone. But if I don't get a chance to write because I'm continually trying to scrape together enough to eat, my hands might as well be cut off and served as "between course" tidbits at the dinner for the Festival of Sleep. "Between course," a marvelous term since cooking came to be considered an art and has needed all its connections between one course and the next, the same as elegant literary style. The guts and every kind of scrap—feet, claws, and vegetable tops, for example—were thrown to people who were starving to death, the peasants. And they invented a single, not very artistic dish for their cuisine: "stew." They survived, but they certainly weren't able to do much thinking about the future. Other heads and other hands, free and well-suited for treachery, thought about it for a little while. They were devoted to writing that had not yet been flattened by the asses of the mass media, as they term it, so these products can be more readily eaten.)

(I notice that my hands are trembling now, as a result of the prolonged exercise of writing, I imagine; this should go away with training. It certainly will if I don't get too hungry. Which will last longer, me or the paper?)

Day Ten

I was never on the inside. I never linked arms with the marchers, but always stayed on the periphery. I watched the last ones from the window, looking down at an angle, and from this distant position I had a chance to measure the growth of hatred in all the others who watched from their windows while keeping themselves hidden. From behind curtains, between cracks in half-lowered blinds, from balconies—but with one leg in and one out, so they could make a quick retreat. If these watchers had been able, they'd have killed the marchers on the spot, but they were conditioned by a culture accustomed to homicide by proxy, discreet and gray if at all possible. They used the vibrations of hatred as conduits through the silence of the boulevards and back streets. The intensity of the vibrations could be measured by the fixity of the stares and the increasingly marked pursing of lips by those who disappeared back into their houses.

I had a strong desire to stop those marches, or at least redirect them to a better world. In the real one, where they were taking place, broken shopwindows (whose monetary value everyone knew) were more important than the people who were killed. They acted like they deserved what they got and human life didn't mean a thing; it just meant fewer mouths to feed. This is culture at its lowest possible level. The feelings that filled me were so intense I was overwhelmed with rhetoric, and goose bumps covered my motionless, paralyzed body. My ancestral hair stood straight out on my back and the hair on my head froze at the roots. The parade of red banners, a symbolic multitude within a multitude, made this state even more intense, if that was possible. It stirred the spectators so strongly (they were unfed and therefore starving with hatred) it made them feel they were a part of the moment and freed the intense emotion you sense only in the theater, where you see the truths of life being staged. There you really experience the actions and passions of life, while if you meet them suddenly, naked and raw, in the course of your daily existence, they have no effect on your normal state of dullness. So it is necessary to record and project in order to understand and eventually to feel compassion, even if you have to change the speed at which things are happening by using devices popularized by the movies, like slow motion takes (almost always a replay). We keep going back to look at the same photograph again and again, mental or actually printed, trying to put memories into action, drawing new connections and interconnections from the memory's storeroom, small but critical variations, mute or spoken.

In dreams you burst into sobs which send you to the brink of life and death, and in dreams you unleash orgasms far more powerful than the ones you experience when you're awake.

The parades of young people had now entered into the phase of cinema about itself, then of cinema actually made from cinema. Maybe this is better: theatrical repertory with that certain amount of enthusiasm and participation a theater has when its actors never get tired and can renew themselves constantly; that an acting troupe has when it can renew itself by substituting the old and tired with new adepts who carry very small but vital modifications. But in this cult of the theater, in this tentative balance between pretense and reality, present and future, *the others* (those representatives of hatred) were also important, and they prepared the massacre because they knew how to manipulate those delicate mechanisms. In fact, the carnage which ended the game was carried out on two complementary and interconnected levels. There was the level of maximum reflex horror, which could only be properly conveyed with theatrical blood, in technicolor, and thus offered maximum satisfaction in the hateful volley of gunfire. The other was the level of devalued reality: everything is theater, it's all put on, allowing us to accept it all without fear, after ridding ourselves of the suspicion that it was indeed real, that it was lambs to the slaughterhouse. They all seem dead, but it matters little to know if they are or not. And if they are, we remove them quickly, making use of the catharsis for all it's worth. Like destroying an old couch we've made love on, and then finding it at our feet in a moment of regret, of exhaustion without relief, stomach tied in knots.

The final signal was given by someone who had most acutely followed the evolution of the performance, not very long after the addition of the Indian mimes. With the excessive language of their gestures, filled with revelations and outrageous acts, always insulting to bourgeois morality, they quickly conquered even the most seasoned veterans. They all began to think they really did live on a Reservation, where even pistols and Molotov cocktails were tolerated for certain brief parts of the performances. It seemed like a way out, a means of redemption. A stroke of vitality, of invention, and it would have continued that way if they had not taken the decisive step toward that total theater which has been a dream of so many, including stubborn actors, throughout this century. Behind the stage there was a tomb, a mass grave (and I'm not talking about symbols).

The madness of the whole thing finally overwhelmed any remaining sense of reality or the real world, and the free fall toward the Performance could no longer be stopped. The Final Scene, the one that always moves us to tears, was announced suddenly by the rapid fire of automatic rifles, together with slashing sabres from the reconstituted cavalry, the small cannons of armored cars, hand grenades. The Date chosen for the debut and the closing, in this case the same one, was the day of the demonstration for the democratic army. They had joined together with them in the call for unilateral and progressive disarmament. The Indians were authorized to carry out a symbolic occupation first, and then the rest joined them en masse in the legendary Grand Piazza, with its many well-controlled access streets and high buildings on all four sides. The sharp-shooters gave the signal to open fire at the moment they began to distribute food. In the finale there were bayonets for the wounded and grenades for ambulances foolish enough to answer the call.

(It's threatening rain, and I'm afraid I'll have to take shelter in the storeroom. Mice scare me. There isn't anyone who doesn't think that if he falls asleep in the midst of them they won't slip up his asshole and hollow him out from the inside with their claws and little teeth.)

(A stranger who was passing by, a boy, told me that a survivor of those torturing vigilantes called the "special corps" was recognized and got his throat cut. They strung him up by his legs like a pig when you want to drain its blood. The practice of cannibalism is starting up again: I saw them with my own eyes, he said. I was well hidden, like an explorer in the old days, with my hair standing on end. Having satisfied their thirst for revenge, these man-eaters want to take on the power of the people they eat. In this constant of cannibalism, our last "little hopes" seem to sink, certainly those called "short term," a definition popularized by the old capitalists with the obtuse memories of vampires, sorcerers more than cannibals, alchemists who could transform human meat into paper money. He also says the cannibals, like the last old capitalists they managed to catch, were buried alive, at least the ones who were caught in the act.)

(I found the old thief dead. He's through crawling around on his hands and knees. I set him up in the wax museum with a full can of tomatoes in one hand and a sharpened spoon in the other, sitting on the ground. Some sugar cubes around him to attract the mice, who attack the face first because it's uncovered.)

Day Eleven

I'm looking to see if there's anything left in my wallet, where I often put a little bit of everything, not just money. Pieces of paper with addresses and telephone numbers, newspaper clippings, and these not following a system (from there they were periodically transferred to my files) but just chance, or so it seemed. We know nothing happens by chance. (But this excessive use of the verb *to know* to explain an acquisition which came before the present discourse, isn't it an alibi, the dribbling of a lazy, slothful intelligence? Yes, it's an alibi: as I write I realize how little I knew before I started to write, before I began to put this presumed knowledge to use.) So we must suppose the clippings were, for me as a reader of daily newspapers, what they call focal points, points where many lines drawn from my thoughts and reflections intersected. I believe this one stayed in my wallet because I wanted to read it again before putting it away. Or read it to some friends. Maybe because of its odd nineteenth century title, which is at the same time so up-to-date: "A Tragedy of Poverty." At least now I'll be able to read it for a specific reason: it describes a manner of behavior, when confronted by hunger, that served as a model followed by small masses of my ex-fellow-citizens.

Bologna, March 12. She was found with a pistol, shot through the heart, next to a pile of garbage. She had been dead for some hours. The suicide [or murder, *ed.*] occurred at two o'clock last night in a farm house on the outskirts of the city, in Vicolo dei Prati. The dead woman, whose name was Enrica, was twenty years old. Last night she was hospitalized at the Maternity Institute because of a miscarriage. The pistol was made in Belgium. Yesterday evening she stayed up late with a friend who also lives in the little shanty on the Vicolo dei Prati; around two in the morning she suddenly went out and shot herself in the heart. This is the young man's story and it could not be disproved by a paraffin test of his glove. The police are trying to ascertain if any of the seven citizens who live in the shanty next door heard the pistol shot. The coroner has an opposing view. He claims—it is not clear on what basis and with what likelihood—the girl's death preceded the shot in the heart. No matter what the circumstances, this was a tragedy of poverty. The girl and her man were entirely lacking in means. She had scraped together a little money by working as an assistant hairdresser for several months, and he by doing odd jobs, mostly criminal in nature. They said they wanted to get married but that they couldn't even think about a house. Perhaps the other evening Enrica, hearing "no" said one more time, found the strength to take her own life. They found her sitting with her head resting on her right shoulder.

This happened in the not so distant Year of Our Lord 1976. It was not long afterward that such actions became a frequent way of responding to life. Pistols randomly thrown out all over the place by soldiers, by special corps vigilantes, by guerillas, out of streetcars, out of trains, from moving busses: and so the means for putting an end to hunger came into many people's hands completely without cost. Tentative sporadic beginnings, and then it was practically a daily occurrence. Done in solitude, as is appropriate for a self-inflicted gunshot, a little to one side, around the corner, behind a bush. They no longer recorded waste removal statistics (what happened to the sewerage technicians who took the census of the City's inhabitants, in the month of

August for example, by measuring the level of shit?) and no one bothered to record the pistol shots of suicides.

(Ate smoked herring that were hidden under . . . now I forget. They made me incredibly thirsty and so I got half drunk and started to worry over how I write. It was as if I were writing with a chicken's foot. Will I be able to decipher it later, read it myself? I could do with a little less wine. "It's old people, in general, who get drunk," I once told a little nephew of mine with absolute confidence some years ago. I'm worried about them, these almost indecipherable lines, like a clown who pretends to worry in a drunken way about being a clown. . . .)

Day Twelve

I'll start this with a note on young people (the last one? don't bet on it). They proclaimed everywhere—through all the media, including official State radio, and always early in the morning—that "they had rejected the logic of sacrifice," hence the raids against austerity measures, etc. Now in the work camps (mostly concerned with training in farming and animal-raising) you tell me you're thinking about that rejection, how it turned out to be a political mistake, etc. That so many ended up in the camps all the same, and this the logical and correct conclusion to the little apocalypses which occurred day after day: enjoy yourself now, because tomorrow you'll be in the cadres . . . that they had the omen of the grand historical apocalypse right before them all the time, the one that begins with the murmuring of these simple words: "the lights have all gone out. . . ."

Now you consider the camps a *blessing* because they guarantee—or at least they promise—you'll survive. Like a grotesque mirror image of the old German labor camps, if it were not for one fundamental difference: now the weakest come to be helped, while back then they were the first to die. No enclosing fences (except for the ones needed to protect them from animals, naturally) and no movies. But didactic theater has made a comeback, to show people *how* to do things . . . and a simple comic theater to make fun of the clumsy and inept. . . .

An idyllic picture, full of hope, and not to be believed. In fact, I don't believe it; after sunset I see the knives flashing in the shadows. The last remnants of our violent culture? We'll see.

(Didn't digest the half-raw, half-burned rabbit. Someone once told me he had eaten a rabbit's skin in Germany to keep from starving to death. And the hair too? Germany, the heart of old Europe and the birthplace of the labor camps: but the words are only linked together—labor and camp—to indicate opposing realities, as they say. And then over those camps, on top of that monstrous old hairy heart, grass grew and little girls rode their bikes and ran their dogs. But if you listen carefully, if you put your ear right down to the ground, you can still hear the gnashing of teeth. And you always will.)

(Coffee made over an open fire. And almost all of it turned out ok! Changed the sealing ring on the espresso coffee maker and I still have three left. Another way to measure time, along with the sheets of paper I use up.)

Modena, December 4. This morning the central piazza filled up in just a few minutes when the young extraparliamentary leftists displayed sheets on the city hall colonnade and on the side of the cathedral. Immediately afterwards they distributed leaflets that denounced the violations of space provisions and the construction of highly profitable buildings in areas designated as public green zones or restricted to public housing. All programs that now seem never to have existed.

This form of protest was called "sheeting." It recalled the custom of hanging a bloody sheet from the balcony the morning after the wedding night to proclaim the virginity of the bride. And wasn't the act of taking away a person's home the deepest, most intimate violation? A deflowering of another sort?

They hung up the sheets and the crowd gathered. White sheets, but they were not a signal for surrender; they were a call to battle. They brought movies to mind, where everyone wants to look at the screen and see the minimal prosperity that is supposed to be the reward for a simple "respect for the law"; the mattresses of the evicted getting soaked in the rain, respecting the law. But these hopeful words (respect and law) covered a quite opposite reality (and a black one) that the fluttering of sheets tried to drag out of the secret place where crimes are jealously hidden. Because the law doesn't have to be enforced if the powers that be choose not to enforce it; they simply suspend it, and that gives them ample room for its profitable violation.

And so here I am right now, fluttering a few sheets of paper.

Citizen participation was reduced to a minimum (there was absolutely zero of "everyone having his say") in the bumbling that went on in the decentralized governmental structures, while the centralized ones continued to do a fine job of pulling all the strings, and naturally there was nothing anyone could do. One response was to believe that the idle chatter on the radio, on RAI tv, and commercial tv, was a voice. The area of "citizen participation" became so wide that it simply tore itself apart, but without completely destroying itself: a second wave of idle chatter filled the hole torn in the first. The increasing gap between doing things (knowing how to do them, even knowing *how* to use your hands!) and saying them became unbridgeable. As the compass spread right before your eyes its legs went off the diagram and even off the page, on a course toward infinitude. The result was a society incapable of changing itself through this "festival of talk."

If we didn't all die of hunger right away, or within a few months, we owe it to a race of bumpkins, like the farmers who keep getting older and older, and yet there is no one to step in and take their place. Or like the bakers who get up in the middle of the night, and who have continued to work quietly along as utopias have popped up—poisonous mushrooms that only seem to be edible, that simply having been enunciated need slaves trained in food preparation.

Finally silence smashed verbal participation to pieces, destroying that apparent field of discussion, throwing its participants into the necessity of actually doing something, whether that led to life or to death.

To life for someone who had the strength to go on and who succeeded by virtue of solidarity, however minimal (the guy who knew how to start a fire when it was raining attracted everyone who was soaking wet, and they stuck with him). And to death when certain groups joined together in the areas of catastrophes (sometimes an entire district of the city, where before they hardly said hello to each other) and began to practice what had previously been known only as animal behavior: mass, collective suicide. Doing it with a pistol retained certain characteristics of individual action, intimate if somewhat diffuse. But this was a new stage.

Before setting up camp here by the peaceful Lambro I spent several days in a park on the Ticino, a river too rapid and bad-tempered to let you live by it. Hiding behind some bushes, because I was afraid I might get dragged into the situation, I saw a small community or group of people—I cannot be sure—both nude and fully clothed, throwing themselves into the water and then disappearing. It didn't make any difference whether they knew how to swim or not: the current was too strong and they threw themselves off the pontoon bridge right in the middle of the river. This part of the river quickly became the preferred place to die together, because word had gotten around about other people using it. Some groups came to die there by choice, other groups formed on the spot.

(I took the hatchet and split the half-burned rabbit's head in two. Then I licked out the brains, the way I used to when I was a kid, and as I continued to do as an adult with fried birds. "The best part," they told me, sucking out the little skulls.)

Day Thirteen

It was about dawn, and I was sleeping in because I'd gotten to bed late, when I heard this hissing in my ear: "No exploding pencils around, don't worry, no microbombs in fountain pens, in dolls' stomachs, with the detonator stuck through the belly button. No sirree! Nothing left this time; we'll have to do without mutilated little bodies . . ."

"Are you crazy? What time is it?" I said. "And who the hell are you?"

It was as if he had spoken on the run and disappeared with his whispering voice. Then I got up and stuck my head out the opening I use as a door and said in a loud voice, to keep him from going (even though I couldn't see him): "There weren't supposed to be any plantings this year and yet last night the mirrors of the rice fields shined. Who was it? Who managed to do it? Have you seen it too? No one has gone by for days. I haven't been able to see anyone, not even far away, not even when I hide!"

Then I sat down and began to think about how the first green shoots would be coming up in a few days; tender vegetable down swaying in the breeze. I'd stick my hands into the mud in the ditches they dig at the edges of the rice fields and I'd be able to catch tenches. I saw them do it in the Bassa area, and it didn't seem too hard. They told me you have to stand there, holding your hands very still, until the tench brushes your hand with its tail and then you throw it up on the grass. You let them live so they'll stay fresh. They'll keep there for up to twenty-four hours, motionless but alive.

And if he really heard me say that the mirrors of the rice fields shined last night? No, I'm not ashamed. They did shine.

"The last few leaves hang on refusing to die, to fall off, but then they do fall and only a few rare ones make it through the winter, attached but dead, and are finally eliminated by Mutation. And so it went with our last hopes (but a 'so' without the final metamorphosis, without replacement), the last whispers heard at Eastern Europe's silent and transparent wall. I wanted to remind you, now, how hope made us unwilling to believe the immense cube of ice had descended on our plain. And we were unwilling to believe those voices that kept telling the same stories: it seemed fingers and toes fell off from the cold, then entire hands and feet. . . ."

"That winter was so cold the Appennine forests in the valleys around P. turned to ice. The trees split, giving off sounds like a harmonic instrument that ends up going beyond what your nerves can tolerate, and after prolonged exposure drives you crazy, so you've got to stop playing it. . . . And voices seem to come from the ice; they sound like weak moaning. . . ."

The facts about Poland, here's what I wanted to talk to you about: starting with images that appear to be distinct, and their distance explains the difficulty of talking about them, of telling you about them all over again. It's certain they've produced irreversible political aphasias and have thus increased the necessity of talking about them. If I didn't have the strength to do it,

I would have stopped writing long ago, or so it seems to me.

From the newspaper:

The workers who took part in the protest and strike against the absolutely unbearable rise in prices, caused by the Government, after having been fired, were tried, found guilty and finally set free. When the cycle seemed to have ended and the price rise was momentarily suspended, just when the example of the convicted unemployed workers seemed fair and sufficient as a deterrent, the same workers were tried, found guilty, and then set free for the same offense. It was as if it had never happened, that is, as if they had not already been tried, found guilty and (in almost all cases) set free. The administration of Justice thus reached a circularity peculiar to itself: judicial perpetual motion, a merry-go-round.

The statistics: 195 arrested and held; 130 tortured; 20,000 unemployed ending up in the series of trials, fines, releases, new arrests, new fines . . . It goes without saying that the payment of fines had to be repeated several times, and previous receipts duly stamped at the post office were ignored.

Also from the newspaper:

The machine started up to crush the workers' resistance against rising prices is justly called *infernal*. And because of the deep political division in the country, it seems as if it might be able to continue functioning. In reality there now exist two Parties and two Governments and even two Police Forces that square off against each other in their internal affairs. So there is one person who arrests and another who sets free, one who puts out the warrant demanding payment of fines and another who cancels the fines. This is the only way you can explain the survival of the working class. But you might ask if this dualism doesn't represent the age-old millennial image of good vs. evil, and if it might not be an irreducible constant. The answer has got to be "no." It is the same kind of mechanism as those used in the machines of antiquity, running on the energy produced by the movement of weights and counterbalances. The workers are now conveyed on one plate of the scale, then on the other.

Day Fourteen

Letter No. 7

to train in rationality in questioning
in the way we question language by writing
a seeking poetry a reasoning poetry
not for a sentimental education suitable
to ferocious pigs, homicidal turkeys and buffalos
and so this goes beyond the family, yes far beyond
the place where we get our sentimental education
I took you beyond, it's true, to make you healthy
so you can walk reason oppose
kiss without biting

4/19/76

Letter No. 8

I lived three days in a community of animal families
they all wore muzzles for fear they couldn't control
    themselves
they all went around with bare feet for fear of kicking
the little birds of prey kept their claws hidden under
    their wings
outcries were heard at night and little flames burst out
I, a hunting dog, chased back and forth playfully with
    game
then I ran away barking to beat the band:
they all thought they were human beings

4/19/76

We are liberated. They've liberated us from murderous wealth and prosperity. Behind the horizon of Work the phantom of torture stands ready, and it becomes corporeal at this place or that whenever it's needed, going right to work on flesh and bone. Behind the Samba and Carneval there's a metal ring pierced through both penis and tongue, and an electrical current runs through it. (From a diary: "it seems they'll be torn apart together, penis and tongue.") In front of the electrically charged fence the newest hanging chains, with new motors: there to be seen by all, ready for use, having been quickly put to the test.

Only one paradise has been dreamed of on this earth, and it has been imagined well: the farmer's toil seems light and the soil easy to work; the plow has wings and the rain is only beneficial, the waters well-restrained; and the science of nature builds entire countries. But right at its center the Hole, black like all holes: the work camps, internment sites for the re-education of people who are different, who are beginning to deviate or have already done so. Intimately Chinese in their administration of Terror. A few exemplary deaths, sufficient food—or it may be suddenly and arbitrarily withheld. It could even happen to you, at any moment, even while you're asleep. Watch out! The homosexual hairdresser shot without warning right in the midst of his customers and assistants. One morning he went to the bathroom to wash up, and was waiting to use the toilet, and they left him there in the middle of everything (eyes wide open) for hours, as if no one had seen him. Tiny pockets of pus, even in the cities. "Yesterday they shot eight people in the Piazza Rossa." "Only eight? That's not so many."

Recognizing it: the ecology organizations (with pride: "We're on the move" and others, more honest: "We sell ecology!") left us a little inheritance. They taught groups of people, deprived through no fault of their own, that food comes from the earth (example: potatoes) and milk from cow tits ("milk is an artificial product, like Coca-cola," 27 percent of I don't know how many "made in the USA" students responded in a survey).

They even taught small groups of fake farmers one time (but what time? that of painting or rhetoric?) how to go through the solemn motions of sowing and reaping with ballet movements and choral recitations. With the unforeseen benefit that some of them were saved when the game was over.

And how will my delicate little hands react to contact with the soil? Will frost cover them with deep cuts and unhealable wounds? Stiffened by excessive callousing, will they be able to hold pen and pencil?

A proposal to remake theater, since theater is salvation. At one time peasants were obliged to transport landowners to the theater in sedan-chairs. They were supposed to be entertained by watching them dismantle and reassemble the mechanisms of the Happy Society, or watching them reveal the Unhappy Conscience. But the peasants (the people) fixed their glances elsewhere. Naturally they watched the street theater of starving comics, acrobats and tumblers. The difficult daily exercise of acrobatics was easily reconciled with hunger: the body became pliable in order to feed itself with very little. This theater has survived, continuing down to the present day. Or at least it's probable that it's held out this long, but to prove it we'd need to trace those acrobats and actors, and that won't be easy. First of all, they've lived almost completely hidden, at the periphery of legitimate theater, which was continually undergoing a process of death and revival. I'll make you a bet: they're living in trees and catching fish with their hands.

I did it. First of all I caught it by throwing my jacket over it, then threw my whole body on top of it. It was right there, under my belly. Then cut off its head with my diver's knife. I've never known how to twist their necks, not even during the war, when everyone had to try it—at night, in kitchens overflowing with chicken blood. The farmers' wives turned around and bent over when they did it, showing us nothing but their butts: you couldn't see a thing. I plucked it as I was washing out the blood. Cooked over an open fire, but this time I held it above the flames so it wouldn't burn the way my rabbit did. It suddenly came back to me that this is the way you do it.

Victims of the idea of totality. To finish up my writing day, the buzz of idle chatter they carried on (and why not chat a little even now, sitting under a leafy tree, in the dry coolness of a summer night?) about the genetic behavior of the human species would do just fine. In the dialogue which took place between anthropology and the biological sciences, there was one who argued (a Polish doctor!) that the disintegration of the family, group sex, and other sterile variants of sexual behavior were needed by the Species in order to limit the expansion of its own populations. Apparently Sade had infiltrated the DNA which regulates our behavior. And he supported the conclusion with a postulate on eroticism: that the person who is aroused by these deviancies is more influenced by a death wish than he is by the urge to procreate. Hence more murders than inseminations (Sharon Tate and the Valley of Death), vaginas ripped apart instead of being sprayed with sperm, tits served on platters as between course tidbits at cannibalistic feasts, instead of a milky white flow. Similar arguments took up space in the newspapers. They provoked replies. So another doctor (Italian) informed us in letters to the editor that on the contrary the Year of Our Lord 1976 was very fertile (he worked in a hospital where they kept reliable statistics). It was rare for women not to get pregnant, even those who had waited in vain for years. Then what does the Species want? To multiply its population in view of a predictable catastrophe and thereby increase the probability of its survival? Isn't it necessary to recognize that the Species has at least two faces, that it is like Janus? Maybe even three. On the one hand it lets you set up the catastrophe by refining Military Technology and reserving all technical progress for the pre-eminent use of the military and, on the other hand, it swells birthrate statistics by producing an increased desire for sexual activity which leads to fertilization. . . .

(Having wasted away to the bone, this survivor will have the strength to disappear with dignity, knowing that the Species will thereby gain an advantage. Or will I stay alive by transforming myself little by little into an animal—so I can be freed one day by a beauty who will agree to marry me as a toad because I have kept my good heart? For the moment I have decided to set up a reserve: three pens and two reams of paper, untouchable.)

But there's the monster's third face: eternal sexual self-satisfaction. A totally *physical* satisfaction, as the interviewees said. The body needs itself most of all; it needs to feel itself. With others you have to worry about their desires. "Better by myself, I'm more free, less inhibited, more excited . . ." Hands-on demonstrations: orgasm is only clitoral. So lesbians don't hate themselves the way gays do. The latter are always ready to crack themselves over the head with any bronze statuette within reach. Always somebody else's fault. Pursued by the blackmailing three-faced Species: procreate. No metaphysics: the Species is the Law.

And late on this chilly night, the idea for the next report from the farmhouse: the difference between Law and system, or are they really the same? When saying is doing . . . that's army talk. Or should I go out and look for a woman, even in this cold weather. . . . And say to her: "Hey you!" Even if she escapes, she can't escape, and I can't catch her either. At this stage I'm not very fast, and she might turn around and bite me.

Day Fifteen

Milan sparkling in the distance on a clear night was another image that had been erased from recent memory to find its place in the continuum of history, according to the plan that moves us into the future. The effluvia of summer continued to expand, and whoever could went home and made love without holding back.

On a night like this these words come to mind: celestial palpitation, milky body, night without night. If you pay attention you see how they are erased by the sun, little by little or quickly, like the celestial bodies that point with their brief fire. Or if you keep quiet and stop scratching your pen across the paper, questions and answers cease to exist. The margins disappear. The body is self-contained, materiality without aura; questions and answers don't exist outside its dominion. It is there. It doesn't ask, it doesn't answer. It throbs, even if it doesn't have a fever; it bends with the wind.

The difference between a dog and a wolf, between a wildcat and a domestic one. As a domestic dog, I spend most of my time on a chain. Others have managed to break the chain, but they still feel its presence, like the missing limb after an amputation. It's a difference that shows up in the tracks they leave: let's look at the illustration I have here. When the wolf walks, it articulates its paws along a precise straight line, while the dog goes forward as if it were half-drunk, zig-zagging, ready to take to any direction whatsoever; it is trainable, humanoid. So the chain is its only source of stability; at least it offers the coherence of duty.

Wolves or Dogs?

by Gianni Popoli

Some animals have traditionally been considered harmful; among these are the wolf and the wildcat. Then, in a more just action, they were included on the list of protected species because they were in danger of extinction. The wolf population, according to a recent count, is now around one hundred; the wildcat is nearly extinct. Unfortunately the appeal launched for their protection and the new law in their favor have not succeeded in removing that accumulation of ignorance in the minds of many, too many, that makes them shoulder a double-barrelled shotgun, leave poisoned bait, or set fatal traps for these animals. When I say ignorance I am alluding to the total lack of knowledge which makes, for example, anything that has a long tail, erect ears and four paws a wolf, and anything that meows a wildcat.

It is impossible to know exactly how many wolves there are because of the habitual continuous wandering of this animal; it is here today and tomorrow it will be found over ten kilometers away. Making up for the wolve's scarcity you find many dogs that have gone wild in the Appenines. They plunder flocks, hen houses, and are even dangerous to man. These are sheep dogs which do not follow the flocks when they leave the summer mountain pasture and return to the lowlands. They remain in the mountains and take on wild habits.

Domestic cats that have taken on wild habits are no less dangerous. Usually they are males that have run away from home; they live on small mammals and birds. Unlike the wildcat, they don't fear man; and they are more cruel because they kill to satisfy their instinct more than for hunger. So the good are confused with the bad and the wolf and wildcat pay for crimes never committed.

How can you identify these dogs and cats that have gone wild? Close observation leaves no doubt, but most of the time they appear only for a brief moment. Let us say that the wolf is larger than the common dog; it has a thick tail, a large head with a pronounced frontal bone, and a large mouth with powerful jaws. It is not afraid of man, but it avoids him. When it encounters him,

(1) Wildcat's paw: with the black Nehring spot on its heel. (2) Wildcat's paw: tuft of white hair called the Brandt spot between its claws. (3) Domestic cat's paw: the black band which substitutes for the the Nehring spot. (4) Domestic cat's paw: without the Brandt spot. (5) Wolf tracks. (6) Dog tracks.

the wolf first runs away a certain distance, then it stops for a moment and turns, as if to fix the man's face in its mind. If it is not starving it will not come down from the mountains to hunt, and when it does it is with circumspection and much caution. The only traces it leaves are the remains of its meals and very large, oval-shaped pawprints which are arranged in a straight line. The dog's are small, close together and zigzag.

The wildcat is reluctant to approach human habitation; it lives on common mice, field mice, and small birds. Its distinctive markings are: a large cylindrical tail which is short, ringed and always black on the end; ears with fringe on the tips; a black spot on the heel, called the Nehring spot, which in domestic cats goes all the way to the elbow; a tuft of white hair on the bottom of the paw between the claws called the Brandt spot.

[From "Il Giorno," 1976]

Valéry said all dogs have to be suppressed, and he seemed to think it was possible. He ought to be happy now. They're being eaten.

Day Sixteen

Letter No. 9

I said nothing apocalyptic is normal
today, April 21, 1976, someone wrote "Jews to the
    ovens!" on the wall
which is only a small boil I told you, yes
because I pester you and keep saying the fundamentals
never change and people who say "Jew!" what will
they do when the last Nazi war criminal
lies dead in jail and they're outside without an alibi
pants around their ankles and no more Nazis with the
    original label
to try to hang or keep in the zoo and suddenly
a child poet asks: will they hang themselves?
the answer is "no"; contracts are always favorable to
    the ones
who have written the body of the law

4/22/76

Letter No. 10

when I was just a little over thirty and it seems only
    yesterday
or worse today or even last night when I stood there
    watching them
from the window, those Muti thugs with toy machine
    guns (which
are real) in their hands who keep shouting: "to arms,
we are Fascists" it seems only this morning I saw the
    paper
with a photo of a man—they dug out his chest
with knives, cut out his heart with their blades
the same ones they used two or three hours before and
    two hundred meters away
where I work—and so I keep writing again and again
that there are Nazis here within, piss in every corner
so much I need to use this concrete word
to convey the stink, that there are knives around and
    you
say to me "but the Fascists have pistols" and you
    know
that if they call out *comrade* and you turn they'll
    shoot you: "just as if
it were nothing" but I reply that they always come
    from just one place
their own and they go back there, then why do I keep
    writing you
for this reason only: so I can tell you
that you're completely right not to bother with
those adults/children of us the Fascists keep
even in the Chamber of Deputies as if in a zoo

4/28/76

Even if everyone did display the right symbols and send the right signals (and by *everyone* I mean the struggling social parties, who had tons of money and drugged themselves with the fear of being unemployed and poor, which had come to be known as being "marginalized"), few carried out the analysis to the point of foreseeing and predicting the final solution. Here the phrase "final removal" comes to mind. It's like morphine when you have cancer: you can't get by without it.

On one side the pistols of the police (and in a kind of game between hiding and revelation, the first weapons that were brandished openly were published on the first page of a radical left-wing newspaper as "revelations," but they also served as a threat) and on the other side chains, crowbars, Molotov cocktails and pistols. The latter at this time were being popularized in student manuals as "permitted and necessary." Then the first armored cars and *agents provocateurs*, the switching of sides, travesties, pirate radio stations (previously free lance). So everyone knew and saw (except for brief truces between the clashing parties, which seemed to need a certain rhythm of fighting and resting) that they had embarked on a journey of no return toward the preparatory series of small catastrophes. But they still fooled themselves into thinking the driving mechanism of the conflict might be stopped. Because it was boring to keep thinking in terms of class struggle: whoever did seemed vulgar and crude. Or maybe it was because they thought the victorious class would win again easily, and peace would be restored.

Only one person (and they considered him to be a bit odd and simple-minded) maniacally continued to say that he saw the Mushroom on the horizon, and that the guilty culture only pretended it wasn't there. But he only showed simple-mindedness by being indifferent to the removal of first causes. He never understood that the

Military is the soul of Capitalism; he wanted to fight against the infernal machine and thereby save Mankind, imagining (better to become cats!) that Mankind with a capital M was in fact the soul of the Military.

Laid out on a hill just across the way, one of the *maîtres à penser* had asked that no one disturb the silence of his tomb. He remained in that tomb to make sense of the apparitions of the Other World and to redraw maps ("to photograph stray cattle," the bastards said). Then he rose and came down from the hill with a chamber pot full of steaming excrement, and he turned it into gold right before their eyes. At this point someone asked him (pretending that he hadn't noticed the transformation and the fact that the smell had gotten even worse) for a new political project that would not be just the "usual" reform. The "usual": here the asshole kneeled, because he had used an adjective which was entirely improper for something that had never been given and which was in fact impossible to give. Literally: they didn't give him the gold. So he asked for a Compromise, that reassuring word: everybody in agreement, a few skirmishes and a lot of patience. Instead, they all put silly hats on their heads, in this case also "literally."

For only one day, more precisely for the length of a single morning, the papers said the succession of coups all over the world was a chain of little preparatory explosions. That was just before the press was closed down. In one of these countries the people in charge of the coup got rid of tortured corpses or the leftovers of simple executions by throwing them into the sea from planes. The fishermen who saw corpses rain from the sky spread the news; it soon made a circuit of the globe, even though attempts were made to bury it on back pages. But the weight of the everyday, the struggle for survival, had dulled the people's senses. For those capable of understanding, the news leak functioned as still another threat: they too might become corpses thrown from airplanes.

(Needles run through urethra and rectum.)

(To ascertain the rhythm of pain, measure the intervals. About once every 24 hours, it seems to me. The problem of the N bomb became matter for gossip because they had already decided whether or not they were going to build it. When the intensity increases or the length of intervals decreases, I'll have to think of something other than alcohol, which only makes things worse, or at least that's the way it seems. But isn't it necessary to point out that the industrial plants and houses and warehouses left intact in Germany wouldn't do anyone any good because of the complete lack of trade and consumers? For the first time they'd have been idiotically destroyed en masse. And, in fact, they had noted that. The Neutron bomb is weapon as facade: behind it is an industrial complex reduced to ashes for Kicks, dense ash, impalpable, volatile, sometimes visible sometimes invisible, which arrives in little flickering clouds, light or heavy depending on air pressure and the dampness of the soil, and inedible as well, like war bread made of bran and sawdust. Eating clouds? And who among us has never thought of that?!)

Day Seventeen

Well, I said to myself, I'm at the point where I'm ready to assess the difference (and I mean really feel it) between what I define as looking at life and actual living, and the difference between then and now as well. Then I watched life go by and now I live and that's it. Now every one of my movements is necessary and is done for a reason, which in turn justifies it. There is little difference between brain and body, order and execution. And the body of the brain itself doesn't wander off in unnecessary directions: that is, it wants to live, neither to survive or subvive. We have arrived at the often-invoked truism: daily routine is truth. We have arrived at a state beyond explanation (an amphora is an amphora?), the revelation of the material world.

But writing these words (so this is what writing is for?!), getting ready to discuss things with you, my patient and attentive listeners, in this deserted garage that is stained with the oil of vanished cars, I realize that I have constructed a tiresome lie: in reality I am still not living my life but just looking at it. If I hadn't done so, and with the maximum attention, I would be totally empty, a sack without potatoes, I would stumble, trip over my own feet instead of moving straight ahead, I would end up with my snout in the dirt, neither wolf nor dog, with my hands scraped raw, and during the appropriate season I would fall into the fire as I tried to stir it. It seems unlikely I'll ever really change. The brain functions on its own accord: it gives disobedient orders, it obeys the impulses of opposing cultures, it short-circuits, it tears, it blocks, it freezes.

I have rediscovered (and so my life proceeds through rediscoveries that seem more like discoveries) a small book written by a Chilean prisoner who was locked up in a labor camp and tortured. "A manual for our future," I said when I wrote about it (I earned my living that way back then as well). But I believe I immediately added "a manual already appropriate for the present and for the interpretation of the past as well."

The labor camps as a permanent system of education, collective expropriation for the common good. Is it possible? It sure is, and it's the final transformation of capitalism. Capitalism that isn't there except as an amputated limb, registered once and for all, never to be forgotten. To forget it you'd have to cut off your own head, and nobody would call it suicide. But there's something else to add: without the work produced by labor camps, their components (the producers) would die of hunger. That would have the same end as all the missing soldiers of all wars, and all peaces, where deserts advance to swallow up oases.

Is it possible then for someone to live without watching himself live? The great orgasm has passed like a bad summer thunderstorm, and we're here all set for cannibalism—certain people have already started to practice it. In the flesh, I mean, not just in spirit. Up to this point, and other points we don't yet know, the brain is ready to obey anyone who tortures it to make it submit to the Culture sucked with mother's milk. That Culture is revealed to be cannibalistic too, if it is pulled out into the open, dragged out of its hidden caves. Milk and beatings. Labor camp and chemistry (torture). Suddenly there's this tunnel, this asshole you have to go through, and without hesitation.

Now I have two cats. First one arrived, then the other, a few days apart. I watched them for hours and they watched me. I petted them in turn or together until they went away, quickly or slowly but satisfied. They decided when to go themselves. Did they believe I was some large, almost immobile species of cat? They brought me gifts in exchange for affection: mice, pigeons. I can't bring myself to eat the mice (thank goodness I haven't had to yet), so I leave them to the numerous and efficient colonies of burying-beetles (insects) that carry them away. They bury them with a precise technique, adapted to ensure their preservation by enabling them to nourish themselves with these little corpses in case of a shortage.

To them (the burying-beetles) I will leave my body. I must choose the place for the final disposition as well. I will become something like an apple, a ball in the shape of an apple, or a pear, and this is how I'll be buried, put down under the soft dirt, and be preserved as food. Let's look at these drawings together: substitute me for the mouse and multiply the number of insects needed for the work because of the added weight. I would also like to find a substitute for the term "dead animal" in the explanatory notes: it seems a bit irreverent to me.

There next to the place where I'll be, I imagine a mailbox (hanging from a tree or nailed to its trunk) that functions in reverse: instead of receiving mail, it is used to deliver it to the people who pass by. My letters are addressed to anyone who wants to read them, and someone else will have to provide the mailbox with a new supply. That's assuming lots of people pass by, and that they want to stop under the tree, either standing or curled up against a root, because they want to read me or simply to read anything whatsoever, even little pieces cut out of newspapers. When they no longer stop and the mailbox remains empty, the people who pass by will start to bite each other again. And the dogs will back off a moment before being slaughtered. So the transcription continues.

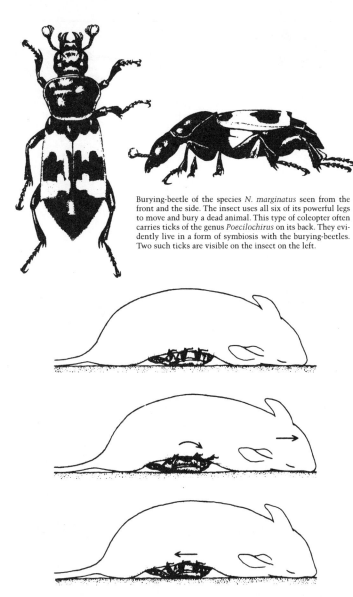

Burying-beetle of the species *N. marginatus* seen from the front and the side. The insect uses all six of its powerful legs to move and bury a dead animal. This type of coleopter often carries ticks of the genus *Poecilochirus* on its back. They evidently live in a form of symbiosis with the burying-beetles. Two such ticks are visible on the insect on the left.

The transport of a dead animal is a technique that the burying-beetles use when the ground where they find the body is too hard. If there is a pair of burying-beetles, they can work cooperatively or separately. They are capable, if necessary, of transporting a small animal for several meters.
[From the magazine "Le Scienze," December 1976]

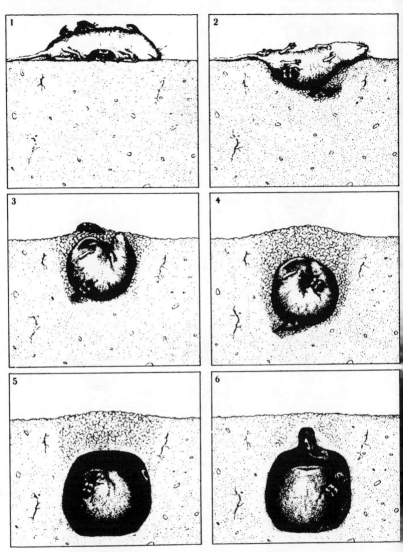

Successive phases of the burial of a mouse by a pair of burying-beetles. Usually a single insect discovers the carrion and then a partner comes to its assistance almost immediately. A male and a female (externally identical) in the process of burying the body of a mouse inside a kind of crypt which is obtained by removing earth and compressing it along the walls and vault. At the end of the operation (6) the dead animal is found several centimeters under the surface. The burying-beetles have transformed the body into an almost spherical form and they have removed the epidermis and the tail. At the top of the sphere they create a small indentation full of liquid food devoted to the use of the larvae, after which the female deposits her eggs in a small chamber dug in the earth just above the indentation.
[From the magazine "Le Scienze," December 1976]

Letter No. 11

while I sit reading at my open window
a horse pulling a cart passes in the street
it has rubber tires for the asphalt where its hooves
beat loudly and bounce around my fourth floor room
while the sound fades and the horse turns the corner
I think of you, around the corner, and I'd like to send
    you
this horse which I imagine to be fat
so you can make it into steaks and store them away

5/15/76

Letter No. 12

free your mind of every thought
look intensely at that white flower
the flower floating on the water
the water is nice and calms the pain
it sinks into itself the water sinks worries and fears
it's like sleep it draws you into its depths
look at the water and let sleep come
because of this dreams gush out to
lift the weight that pulls us under
for this reason sleep is not like
space the difference a word I won't say
now let's continue to look at the water
full of fish with sharp teeth which is life
I'm not writing to you from the sea or a lake
I'm standing before a basin with a nymph
who just happens to be there
as by chance the basin is filled with water
and so I take this opportunity to write you

6/29/76

Letter No. 13

today is June thirtieth nineteen hundred and
 seventy-six
let's pronounce this date syllable by syllable
because we have arrived at this thirtieth of June
nineteen hundred and seventy-six in order to
 pronounce
whispering (but it's a beginning) a word erased from
 History
even though it is the word of the Law: genocide
because we have arrived at this day to make a clear
 decision:
to kill Palestinians with cannon fire
we are in exile, dear Mr. Brecht, we
are here in the midst of all those who pronounce
the word confined to the unspeakable acts of the
 Nazis
and listening to the radio we count them: they say
one thousand a day

Letter No. 14

when I saw a constellation
of drops rain on the page
I dipped my finger in the involuntary
saliva instead of into wine
the red-hot air of recent times blew
unexplored territory where I disembark
this is what I tell myself: it won't hurt
you've got to make the trip anyway
intelligence and dust
beyond my ass I'm screwed

you have to answer me now without making
a blah blah blah noise with your noses

7/5/76

Day Eighteen

Letter No. 15

back home they called him *menschenfresser*
which means "devourer of human beings"
his Christian name was Joachim and Kroll his last
he lived among them but now they say he speaks
in grunts rather than the German language
and further that he trained in the slaughter
of calves and swine so he could get the skill
he needed for his own people. The exact story:

*He was a solitary individual who surrounded himself
with big-breasted rubber dolls and little rag dollies
and every once in a while killed one in bed. He rarely
had complete sexual relations with a woman:
apparently only two times in his life. He's almost
bald and appears clumsy in photographs.*

7/18/76

Letter No. 16

Boves, town with a silly name, the poet Gozzano
    would say
Pieper the name of a little chocolate soldier
Boves, town methodically put to the torch
Pieper shouted the word "fire!"
48 inhabitants got their heads chopped off
today a little more than thirty years have *not* passed
today is yesterday when we awake to the sounds of
    boots
on the streets of Boves and on the second floor
the face of Pieper in terror
his body in flames like all the houses
the dense cloud full of sparks
and the excited minds of children

7/18/76

Letter No. 17

you tell me they've published the photo of the girl
who was beaten, choked, drowned but first raped
with cocks and broom handles now she lies
next to the car where she was held prisoner
the transparent plastic bag they packed her in
pulled down just below her knees
they say she was already dead in the drowning tub
that now once more she lies naked against her will
you might say you want to see this photo
and (I) say it's like repeating the rape
multiplied by four hundred thousand copies and two
million eyes and more every time you pick up the
newspaper and look at her again. . . .

7/21/76

Letter No. 18

I saw the first blood spot on my hand
this morning I said to myself "the time has come"
I sat and stared intently at a piece of wall
and its shining surface I'd like to cut off my hand
it's enough for me to explain my desire to escape
the filthy dream of the stump and write you with that
same hand and make you see it

7/25/76

Day Nineteen

Homo faber. I'm no Robinson Crusoe. I'm not building any kind of future. If I find abandoned utensils, I pick them up, look at them and then throw them aside. To survive I take what others readily give me in exchange, or almost readily. Potatoes that need only peeling. Beans softened by being soaked twenty-four hours and then boiling them. Sometimes I manage to get up and drag myself outside. Then it's a matter of begging, and even if there's something to exchange, I've got to execute these difficult movements: getting myself up and walking. I am confirmed in the opinion my meditation on the difference between watching myself live and actual living is a projection of cultural leftovers, a graph that has no reference to reality, or to what people used to call reality. So much debate on what reality is, "so called" reality. Reality is a potato. When the object is to survive, I just do it and that's all. I lay out plans for little traps, I lay nets of cunning so I can get things. Verbal nets as well. This is how I do it. I reach out my hand and whoever meets me in the desert is forced to stop. In rare cases they run away. I have easily adapted myself to the lack of electricity and have taken advantage of this pleasant time of the year with its longer days. And I have trained myself to read meteorological conditions very well, putting little statistics together with all my memories of past seasons, which come back to me bit by bit. When the days get shorter, I'll put myself into partial hibernation: I'll sleep eighteen hours a day. Or I'll cover myself up with leaves and lie there 24 hours out of 24, as I've imagined I'll be able to do someday so I can finally rest, erasing the image of the resurrection. Desire for darkness, for absence. Having regained my strength under the leaves, I'll burst forth into the new season, transformed. As one who had already started to save on light in the previous life (to lower bills), I was stuck to the window—reading or sewing—down to the last moment. Then I crawled and groped my way into bed, and paused there a moment to look at the darkness, observing the molecular variations, the luminous floating dust, until falling asleep. The blackbirds signal the arrival of light just before daybreak, in the moment that is called "dawn" and the sky lightens but it's not yet morning.

Potatoes and beans, beans and potatoes. Hunger holds us prisoner just as it once made peasants into slaves. Who will ever be able to change this? Whoever has a flock possesses "moveable wealth"; he's the lord of the world. His living money is accepted everywhere, from the tepid seashore to the feet of the great mountain chains, even to the glaciers and valleys. But who has a flock?

I can reflect on snow as an alternative to leaves. Or both together. First leaves, then snow on top. I'll wait for the first snow and, when it comes, quickly stretch myself out under it, and then all the other snows layering up if the weather behaves normally. Underneath it never drops below freezing. Going into hibernation can become the purpose of living nowadays: looking forward to that happy moment. A little before, I'd think about moving a thousand meters or so away to a more favorable spot, not too exposed, where the lightest crystals reappear in the air again and again.

Day Twenty

"... then the turning point, the uncontrollable loss of areas of refuge, and casual destruction, impossible short circuits at the last command headquarters, the almost continuous earthquake from unknown faultlines which had never been marked on the maps that denoted slippage. And suddenly, beyond the bend, the valley opens up, slopes down, renders itself habitable, and a new history begins, the seductive damsel utopia who sings her nightingale verse, and who this time seems completely real. The place that can never exist is right here within reach, just a few steps away. In fact, the weary traveler stops in total disbelief for a moment before continuing on. His destination is so close. He leans on his walking stick, chin on hand, thinking: Class has finally destroyed itself. . . ."

Exhausted, I watch myself fall (on the little stage) into the empty sphere of uselessness. I see toupee and dentures fly away, weightless, and priestly robes and businessmen's suits fall, turning into theatrical dust, with gesticulating hands and a strident voice which can only be guessed at, because in reality I'm no longer uttering words.

"... all the predictions reversed, disproved, fallen into ridicule? It is exactly at this point that I ask myself if the news we've received is trustworthy, if what we believe and say but haven't actually seen has really happened here on the banks of the river. But we still talk about it anyway, here among the trees. Loss of Control? But isn't it exactly this which is the last beachhead of Class, what it always aimed for, maybe out of necessity? Have we forgotten the large and small tactical moves connected with a similar strategy? One moment that is worth all the others: the urban guerilla. The terrorist comrades, employed and killed, martyred and multiplied. Class cannot lose control if it doesn't want to. Class is God. Let's try to hypothesize a Reactionary Masterplan—just so, a divine one, like what we call biological regeneration. It's simpler, more believable; it's limited, without future. It is Class that regenerates itself...."

I'm getting ready to leave you in peace, in a little while. Where have the Doves flown? When we see them gliding above us again (we, the little cannibals), we'll know that Class is alive, olive branch in its beak, singing its song.

(Note to be inserted: baskets full of pistols are scattered all over the place—on the ground, on stairs, in elevators, in storage rooms, for anyone who wants them....)

"... and another example of bad literature, a wall inscription: *Blue Shit*. This should be a sign of someone using his imagination. And gold? The price goes up and shit is colored and maybe it doesn't even stink anymore, like paper money. Blue shit sold in the supermarkets, in glass cases, shining, chilled.

"Little signs that make me afraid nothing has changed, other than the total lack of energy. It was also like this after the Second World War, but only in limited areas and not for very long. Does someone know the answer to this question: who are the survivors? And what parts of the Apparatus have survived? We don't know yet. . . ."

(One night on the autostrada, as I was reading the illuminated billboard advertising *Ceolin Shoes*, I imagined that the lights suddenly went out and I wanted them to. In the dark I had to use the stars to orient myself, but I didn't know how to recognize them. I didn't even know their alphabet, so they were useless to me. I looked at them and that was it, body against body. Your eyes quickly adjust to their weak light, and you find it is penetrating.)

(Reread the little ending piece which precedes this. It seems persuasive but completely useless. Today one of the cats made me the gift of another fieldmouse, just after I got back home. Maybe I should stop sharing my food with them so they'll quit doing this. But wouldn't they keep on giving me fieldmice just to ask for more food?

I'm sure they'll never feed on my body, whereas the fieldmice would not hesitate. Who is more intelligent? Who is less sentimental?)

Day Twenty-One

Letter No. 19

they say there are 17 dead workers not 3
they say there aren't 17 dead workers but only 3
the Polish Regime is ready to deny it they say
the other Communist parties have condemned
the Polish Regime is ready to entrench itself behind
the difference constituted by the number 14
the finger the Polish Regime hides behind
is the number 14 like 14 ghost workers
who enter and exit the stage for a rehearsal
after a moment of unbearable noise silence follows
the stage remains empty

7/27/76

Letter No. 20

they say: this is Zone A *we* who have
showed we know nothing say it and *you*
must believe us if we say: this is Zone B
and you must still believe us if we say: we are wrong
we who know nothing and yet are appointed to know
from now on Zone A and Zone B are unified
previously there were 45 families now there are
    15,000 people
who must report there on our orders as we order you
to follow the medical prescriptions we send in the
    mail
we're in charge and we guarantee they work
it's not our fault no one has died yet
saved for the explosions: get out of here. . . .

7/27/76

Day Twenty-Two

A girl jumps up and mimics the voice of a tough little schoolboy: "let's have a snowball fight." It's night; we're in the country. For a few minutes the proposal is ignored; no one shows any sign of having heard it. Then one by one the adults go out into the courtyard and begin to make snowballs with the fluffy, dry snow, in the courtyard lit only by diffuse light cast from open windows and reflected on the snow. In the soft glimmer of the night faces emerge, disappear, then reappear dodging the snowballs. Between moving and running bodies, mine included, in the precise moment of aiming, the automatic, emotionless repetitions of movement in a young adolescent body, that period which no longer breaks through the successive layers of incrustation. I was just about to tell you a story (one time, after starting to throw snowballs early in the afternoon, night fell without my even realizing it—even the gods play, or rather only the gods play—when I was savagely beaten by my father, who was put into a rage by my mother, who had to be repaid for all the tears caused by my disappearance, and she approved of the consoling punishment that functioned as a tranquilizer or a sedative for the anguish caused by the son who had been lost and now was found—until he shouted: no more, no more, when it was already too late) but instead I will keep quiet. Who would take pleasure in the story of one afternoon in my early adolescence if it no longer stirred emotion even in me, and was triggered by an automatism that seems hackneyed?

Telling it now I imagine myself being delivered sealed up in a refrigerator crate, loaded on top of a truck together with other refrigerators, waiting for the energy to come back, and the truck starts moving again and takes me down to the loading dock of a port, ready to be hoisted onto the ship. This happened one time to a kidnapped child, as the police later revealed. And also in that case a ransom was paid to demonstrate that the body, a human life, has a negotiable value. Inside the crate, meanwhile, you take on the value of the missing refrigerator, at least for the customs officials.

I was ready. That evening I had proof of it. I was already expecting what was later to come, what has now arrived. The certainty that decisions were always going to be made by Others, elsewhere, forced me to look at life as if thunderstruck—it was pure repetition, both in nature and among men. I couldn't do anything about it, trained for dispossession like everyone else. In fact the system of labor camps was just then coming to light, the number of locations multiplying daily: the knowledge of how much had happened stayed alive and therefore had to be buried. To watch over and punish. Punishment after punishment is always the prisoner's due, whoever he may be.

Even now the memory of that night of dry, fluffy snow is upsetting me. The gods existed and they died, dried up like exported little boys. I ask myself if they will rise again, if they still exist, if I'll know how to find them again and show them to you as well, my gentle listeners. The gods breathe into us the sense of what can be seen and touched. A visit from them can destroy the extraneous. Maybe they'll come like a thief in the night. This is what I want to tell you this evening.

Along the striations of cracked plaster
leavened by creeping moisture
in the many natures of ice
that day and night change from one into another
in the preparation of tree bark
in this way, subtly, the mutations show
themselves to us

(So the dawn of the story that follows the night of the story coincides with the real dawn, after a real night, and I can slip off to sleep secure in having seen the beginning of another day.)

No Number

I imagine that this is a holiday, out of the usual calendar, having freed itself from the necessary sequence. I wash up and change clothes and start to write a

Poem Dedicated to Scardanelli

where the tangled threads split
there are gods
where cracks in the ground gather seeds
the gods are there
at the point of disorder
of the infinite possibilities of decision
there are gods
inside the green fuse already lit in the ice
protected by fuzzy down
inside the heavy buds ready to explode
live the gods

where the river plows the earth
and returns on itself
in the sound of pebbles grinding on one another
where a root breaks through and drinks
when the fields worked by men and machines
begin to leaven
then the gods give off their scent

even those that were called celestial
the carriers of oxygen
navigate among us

. . . .

is there a limit to the earth? No
there isn't
not even the celestials believe
there is
and limits, they dare joke,
don't wear clothes

. . . .

when a man enters a room and takes
in his hands the objects he finds
on the table or credenza
and throws them on the floor
grabs well-cooked food
and throws it out the window
to the dogs
the gods have wished it so
in their cruelty
unemotional by definition

. . . .

where there is weariness the gods are absent
when you prepare to settle accounts
with the Lords of the Earth
the gods sharpen weapons and give them to you
they weave heavy hemp ropes
they point out Trees to the people
who spread out like a fan who surge forward
the gods blow at your back

winds become favorable
friction decreases
the velocity of impact is like
a gunshot right between the eyes

. . . .

. . . man lives poetically . . .
the gods shape their lips
into a kiss

. . . . .

   The climax of the kiss is that half of the afternoon when the Festival declines and disappears. Then numerical series and obligatory sequences return, and I have to get ready. With the last light I must transcribe:

Letter No. 21

it was the 30th of last month when I wrote you that a
    few people
were quietly saying the word "genocide" and today
    which is the 30th
of the next month for the first time a nationally
    distributed
newspaper of secular opinion printed the taboo word
in big letters—*genocide*—to tell us what's been
    happening
for a month at Tell El Za'tar where there's been no
    water
for a week: you ask me why did they let thirty days go
    by before
they decided to use the word that best reflects
the intention: because by now the genocide is
    complete or at least
they hope so and thank God for the earthquake in
    China to busy us
with relief for the Chinese and to remove even the
    images
of the wounded left there to die of severed pipelines
of pregnant women pursued to make sure
they never have babies again . . .
if I look into the leaves of the giant alder
elbows on the windowsill the spaces between the
    leaves
fill up with torn ghostly sheets.

7/30/76

Day Twenty-Three

There's an unsatisfying kind of sleep which is more restlessness than rest, where the body seems suspended between contrary forces that stretch it to the breaking point. It is a state producing a kind of rigidity in the limbs, so that in the morning, this morning, I have the impression I am in the middle of a metamorphosis, turning into wood like a puppet, but without the ability marionettes have to articulate and disarticulate at the joints. Human marionettes have it too.

This morning I awoke after this fitful sleep, divided between bodily agitation and intervals that reproduced the deepest anxiety of my dreams: my first thought was that I'd have to move around jerkily like Toto's Pinocchio. But it's hardest at first, when you try to get up on your feet, even when you manage to get up on your hands and knees. So I gave up. I preferred to give in to my lack of strength (hunger has its importance here, but so does the silent landslide of desires produced by isolation), and I stayed flat on my back. At that moment I felt quite clearly that my penis was turning to ice. Warmth returned little by little to other limbs just as it was fleeing from my balls and cock, which were now only a ghost-like presence.

When anxiety got the upper hand and turned into fear, especially when I was a boy, I felt a sensation of intense cold in my balls. And it was as if my penis were missing. Very different from the way I feel this morning, which is almost the contrary: the desire for sexual coldness, and freezing. Which is, it seems to me, my body's attempt to solve an insoluble problem, one I can only resolve in another life.

On my back I thought first (I'm still talking about this morning) of starting to write, since I do that sitting on the ground, hunching over. But the successive stages of freezing would have had the immediate consequence of my sexual apparatus falling off and breaking like delicate blown glass. Or, if it had not fallen off, it would have gone into hibernation. That would have suspended the problem, instead of permanently resolving it. Then the day would come when I'd start trying to determine the stages of thawing. But only in another life, I believe.

Then the voices, the transformation into voices of certain things I'd read, the whisper of confessions written or murmured into other ears, as a persuasive accompaniment to the results of that intense cold. They say males are almost always disappointing because they're obsessed with coitus, and that they're almost always incapable (because of this obsession with penetration) of prolonging the period of excitation as long as desire might wish—and that would be almost infinitely. But in the beautiful moment when the male comes, his anger explodes. His impulse is to kill the moment, insulting it first, rather than to ride it with a joyous shout. But what do I have to do with these gossiping voices? What do they have to do with the desire for my penis to freeze? Nothing.

And yet behind it all there's a loud screeching, a sound so shrill it's almost beyond hearing range. Free abortion: a shout that hides (but not too well) a desire for death along with orgasm, for sterility, for collective harikiri.

This is early in the morning. Around noon, or rather exactly at noon, looking at the rod that doesn't throw a shadow (a memory from childhood) I manage to get up on my feet. From down on all fours I make it up into the erect position, just a little bent over. I feel nimble in the heat and all my musculature seems to be coming alive again, stretching and contracting regularly as I walk. Someone grabs my wrists from behind and puts his mouth to my ear, saying: "But watch out for those women, now. They run in groups of four, six at the most, faster than tired men. After one of them signals the others that she's found something, they dash in, steal all the food they can find, and get away scot free. They're called Girl Scouts." And off he goes at a dead run.

The late afternoon has turned out to be perfectly suited for the transcription of my letters: as preparation for imminent nightfall, as the transformation of my body into sheets of paper. I figured out how to put together a little box with boards, hammer and nails. I have come to:

Letter No. 22

here before me a circle of fire has closed
one evening a circle of fire opened on the hill
pushed along by a strong wind that spread it
scattered smoke all through the night and morning
and the dark circle, the hill of brown ashes . . .
you know this happens every time a man
sets fire to a hill down here in the South to give proof
of oppression and revolt, here where living is closer to
survival: (I) would set fire to the houses as well
if I were a Southerner, I would make my donkey
explode under a bridge like a bomb . . .
but I see it's not only me that's content to live in this
    warm
benevolent and fertile climate and they said
(yes, support for the Italian Communist Party is
    growing)
"I want my grave to be here, where it's dry,"
    emphatically
and I take note: no one here believes he's going to die
these graves are painted as if for life.

In a little while I'll head back on my return trip
if I could have changed skin and liver and intestines
then I'd have stayed but I feel my balls contracting
I have the impression I'm leaving them down here
buried under an oak tree . . .

8/22/76

Letter No. 23

the windows are all closing
(looking inside the houses you
asked: hello, do you have any work?)
the doors are all closing
(pressing a hand on the windowpanes
you asked: hello, do you have a job?)
you wind up and down the Italian peninsula
a long line of ants sprayed with DDT
(but it once was outlawed)
you two are also part
of these formations of the damned
I have given birth to you for this
(now I give you money to survive)
I put my shoulder to the wheel for this
(at closed doors, closed windows)
they tell you: go try farming
while others flee from the fields
(I will continue to give you money)
they flee the drought, the hail, the markets
(but one day I won't be here anymore, you know that)
a gulp of water at a fountain (it's good)
the begging begins again
they try to pass single file over the Alps
(Bel Paese is a cheese made from skimmed milk)

8/24/76

Letter No. 24

(popular song here in the South)
Jesus Christ's beard
is not God's beard
everyone knows that
but they still sing his wounds here
they play the tambourine with his nails
they crown themselves with his thorns
they dance shaking his robe
they tear his man's beard from his face
they all know he's a man like them
religion is a foot on the neck
a stomach stabbed by a knife
wine comes from the wounds
spit from the mouth

8/26/76

Teeth grinding and flashing at the same time in the deep starlight. A meter away from me, one hour ago (and I'm writing by the light of two candles: there are two more packs of them). Thick curly hair (I touched it for an instant) and fixed, yellow eyes. Short fur and immediate flight, with a sort of yelp articulated into words. Very quick, like a beast on all fours, yet bent forward like a sprinter, who doesn't stand straight but stretches forward throughout the race. A scampering flight, more like a monkey's. It's hunger.

Man cannot become a fish or a merman: they've scraped the traces of this ancestor off the nervous system, but not of the wolf. When all the circumstances are favorable, it can happen: in the thick of the forest, here at the crest of the mammalian hill. Are there many of these around now? Nobody has ever gotten close enough to touch one, and nobody has seen one from a distance either. Shadows moving quickly through the trees could be anything, even movements of darkness and light, visual distortions.

I put a plastic plate of unsalted crackers ten meters away from my den. In the nocturnal silence, among the thousand rushing noises, I thought I heard the sound of chewing, saliva being sucked up. There's water in a cup right next to the plate, but it can drink from the river. In fact, it didn't drink it. The cup remained full.

Day Twenty-Six

I got ready for the trip by inspiring myself with the image, reproduced in thousands of prints, of the pilgrim with his staff and bundle, bindings around his legs to protect against brambles and insects, floppy hat and nose pointed straight ahead. Also a little hunched over, as I am when I write.

Purpose of the trip, to satisfy my idle curiosity: to find out what happened to an autonomous group that abandoned the city some time ago in an attempt to make itself completely independent and self-sufficient. Autonomy for them meant ending all compromise with political power by taking action that was no longer just a symbolic protest against the dominant culture, but was also practical and material. The obligatory choice was farming and animal rearing. With a modest amount of start-up capital, it's not difficult to try this, since so many have simply abandoned the earth.

First I took several turns around the storeroom to orient myself, like a migratory bird. It was also to stretch my legs, and it worked just fine; I'm better moving than staying still. Then I was off and on my way. I knew they couldn't be far: they'd be there on the first hilly slopes lapped by the Lambro, where certain pieces of land remain like islands in the middle of Northern Lombardy's chemical devastation. In all, only three days from here, round trip. I didn't stop there for more than a few hours, because there wasn't anybody around anymore. Only the signs of work that had been left not too long ago, and dried excrement, and the bones of devoured animals, chicken feathers blowing in the breeze. It looked like the movie version of a village after it's been sacked.

I stopped, leaned on my long fake nomad's staff, looked at a wall filled with writing, with shreds of pasted up newspapers. I realized I should have been able to see where the whole thing would end up, predicting the inevitable result. But the stimulus of my little trip, even the movement itself, had value nonetheless. It was good to actually touch things with my hand. The experiment had therefore succeeded, in this ruined state, in demonstrating the physical impossibility of a separate society. They left here because the soil was played out and the biological reclamation was insufficient for the requirements of this restricted community. So portions of land (some still rich, or at least less impoverished than this one) will continue to be overworked until the land's continuity is broken forever. Or, alternatively, a preindustrial society will spring up—and this can't be excluded as one of the possible hypotheses.

All these thoughts as I was standing there, protecting my hair from the wind by pulling my hat down to my ears. A menacing bank of clouds was moving down from the precipitous mountains, and that gave me a shove, a kick in the ass, to start me heading home. On the way I was on the lookout to see if I would run into anyone. And I often had the impression there was someone going my way, hurrying to hide himself behind the nearest tree or lying down in the tall, rustling and uncut grass.

Here's the fake nomad retracing his steps. They say that in Spain during the *siglo de oro* there were one hundred and fifty thousand picaros who wandered around, living off the scraps of the wealthy few. These were the infamous nomads, the clowns of the lowest nobility in both countryside and capital. But one day I dreamed of a different kind of nomad, one like the Tuaregs. I was thinking that the desert, their homeland, was not a desert at all. In it women and men searched for and found (though with great difficulty and only because of their extraordinary ability to adapt) there were blue and beautiful places where it was possible to live. Water wells, reserves left by rare rains. Every one of them transmitting his itinerary to every other. The women played violins through the night.

But was there ever any culture that supported autonomy, if not a subordinate one, which was therefore subservient to the rejected society? And wasn't the first consequence that they bared their throats to the executioners, offering them victims who are really accomplices and necessary for the persecutor to exist?

I took the bindings off my legs, my dear potential attentive listeners, bindings loaded with thorns and fleas that I quickly burned. Now I am waiting for someone to answer my questions. While I wait I'll read you a piece from a newspaper I tore off the wall in the barren village. Autonomy as a separate movement which elaborates, in that maximum point of resistance, the project of the revolutionary society. It's an error that is called utopia; the work produced within a capitalist society for the purpose of its slow and progressive transformation is always called servile.

If they take two horses, tie a rope to each one and the loose ends to a man's two legs, send them galloping off in opposite directions, the effect is less lacerating than this. A pompous, archaic image that means I can't give you an answer.

This is how my little trip ended, my intrusion into the heart of utopia.

Day Twenty-Seven

Letter No. 25

if you need oxygen read B.B.
Listen to this! "My arm is fucked!"
"and the bandages, where the hell are they?" No,
    Mother Courage
doesn't move and Kattrin threatens Her Mother
with a stick the Howling Menace pulls out shirts
rummages in the debris and starts to suckle a
    wounded baby
which she tosses aside when she sees a soldier trying
to take off with her bottle of brandy and then
Mother Courage tears the fur coat off his back, saying:
Animal! there's another wounded person down there,
Now Pay! A whistle from below and Kattrin escapes
with her red boots through the snow
that starts to fall at the end of the Third Act . . .
If you need oxygen play the tambourine on the roof!

9/4/76

If there weren't the problem of my diminishing strength, I'd take a little walk every day, but no more little expeditions. In fact, just this morning a casual but miraculous encounter. I met a boy who said one day in my car: "the pistoleros have arrived" and I in response "then they're going to fuck up the whole movement." "That's the whole idea; we've got to do something." In that generic "something," no one could have foretold (the pistoleros went anywhere they wanted to, overtime, except in the factories where the guards and managerial defense squads worked) that they'd bring down everyone.

I got tired trying to catch up with him, because the boy kept walking hard and didn't seem to want to stop. But as I ran along by his side, I heard him say: "They're selling slaves again, and they're calling them *free* because everyone can decide whether he wants to be a slave or whether he wants to starve to death. This new kind of slavery has its advantages: you eat, not too much, but you eat." I don't give up on trying to explain things to him: "But you know men are always bought and sold, you know the word *emo* originally referred not only to men and women, but also to things and animals . . . hence the word emolument, which means the same thing in the most servile labor. . . ." "So now there's no misunderstanding; you put yourself directly on the market, rather than through an employment agency . . . no?" I'm breathless from my little run, and I stop with the conviction I've just seen a sequence from a Woody Allen movie.

I want to propose myself to the community that will arise in the future as a breeder and keeper of dogs (for hunting and good company) and cats (who can confront arrogant mice and be good companions too). Finally a really good idea introduced into the structure of the emerging society. You can write poems about them in your calmer moments, females curled up asleep and tranquil males. Being a dog keeper could bring you prestige, and sometimes you might even make yourself heard.

In a Nation overrun by funeral processions, everyone is armed, everyone defends himself by shooting it out. The ones who aren't shooting, and instead continue to talk, serve as accompanists to the obsequies. These chattering crickets are crushed under iron heels. An insect must have made its nest in my ear. It keeps buzzing this little phrase: the unspeakable truth of madness. Enough.

Day Twenty-Eight

Children play in the giant cement cylinders of the big conduits, threading their way from one to the other for hundreds of meters. The smallest ones run through bent over at the waist, the larger crawl on all fours. Happiness is making it to the light at the other end of the tunnel, defecation and birth. During the war, the Second World War that is, children used them to get away from the machine-gunning airplanes: to come out again was a rebirth, quite literally. Now they say the conduits have an educational value, that they satisfy unconfessable compulsions that would horrify their respectable parents.

As an adult one of my games was imagining an accident, a kind of suicide. Crashing through a curve on a motorcycle, ending up under the wheels of a city bus, falling from a bridge in a car. And I directed the whole thing with the determination of a dream, concentrating hard as if I stood there pointing. An internal tic, an alarm clock, instantly brought me back to reality, and I walked away from present danger—because the curve really was there, and the bus and the bridge were too.

Then the second part of the game begins: I take up my life again from that perspective, having escaped death, having rejected suicide. Life as an "after," as it is also a "now." Suddenly I became calm and troubles vanished with the sound of my regular breathing. The risk was in the possibility I wouldn't be able to control the advancing suicidal hypnosis, tumbling inside without finding the strength to get away. Sinking into the unspeakable dark sleep, instead of waking up. But it is precisely the certainty that the passage is impossible that brings life back. If instead you start believing that the passage is possible, there is a high risk of crossing over into the shadow zone. Then you believe you can pass from life/death to death/life, and unhappiness can't push you any farther than that. But training yourself to run away from death is part of a good education, which is exactly what has been given to me. I was loaded up with it by my father, who tried or pretended to try to kill me with his bare hands. In my early childhood his favorite game was to smother me with a feather pillow on the big double bed. And suffocation was whirling there inside the feathers. The same thing happens even now to the children who defend themselves with pistols.

I saved this clipping from the paper, and I transcribe it in its entirety:

Belluno, March 20. Almost eleven years after the flood of 1966, the waters of Cortolei creek have returned one of its victims. Even if identification is not yet official, it's certain that it is Angelo Ritorti: it was his son Angelo, 27 years old, a fishing enthusiast, who found him this morning on the first day of the fishing season.

Angelo Ritorti, the son, said he had gone to the creek to fish when he saw a floating body. He ran to the carabinieri to tell them about it and the officers immediately set about pulling the cadaver to the bank. It was still completely dressed and in a good state of preservation, having been saponified or turned into soap. It was the father.

It seems to me that we can draw a lesson concerning this relationship from theology. A lesson with very deep roots. The Father sends the Son to be sacrificed. It's the death of the son that must open the future, the *I will make everything new*. Because the father is already dead, and even if he were to put himself on the cross, he would not redeem the past. Therefore the cruelty of the father seems a necessity throughout man's history, even though the troubles have all been caused by him, by that past which needs to be destroyed. The death of the son is the price of a future. Thus, a possible succession becomes a circle that never opens, and not one link of the chain can be broken. The future doesn't begin; it has already ended beforehand. The din of history risks remaining a closed circuit. To get out of it there is only one hope: it is the father who must be destroyed.

Letter No. 26

Through his poetry if you wish to know him
common man says: he went for a swim
plunged into the river because it irrigates the
    countryside
he says: remember, it's the earth that provides what
    you eat
the farmer's labor is worth more than anyone else's
if you want to hear him listen to his most ancient
    words
he used the "classical style" they say with a smile
he used the country style, the river's style
in the mountains he began to write: "when you see
red fluttering capes you will have a sunny day"
favoring the poets he thought of a day of harmonies
music transfused through the beating of syllables
that it might have cost blood dripping like sweat
    matters little
he said: in the eyes of Heaven there are no obstacles,
if the goddesses return they will overflow from the
    lakes
from the well-made riverbed. Yes, he wanted to divert
    the clouds
ten minutes of hail signal the end of a life
then he exchanged verses drinking tea with a friend
"next year the harvest will be more plentiful"
he trusted in the gods, he believed he could pass on to
    another life
common men ask themselves: who will command
    now?
the uncommon answer is: "no one." People
was the name of the dream: he noticed the sound of
    wounds

without awakening and the enemies he wanted to
    drive back into the sea:
now we begin to breathe the air of the End.

9/10/76

Day Twenty-Nine

Behind the gods (or in front of them) live the monsters that block the way, the gods of hell, projections of anxiety, defecation of fears. Whoever is about to cross into unknown territory knows in his heart monsters are there. If we dive into the sea without fear of sirens, because we think they're no longer hostile, the sooner we fear the lightless depths because of marine reptiles, poisonous fish. We expect to see a giant descend from a mist-wrapped mountain, maybe Polyphemus himself, with lightning flashing from his one brilliant eye. Fauns don't scare us like sirens; however, we do fear an encounter with Scylla. She has a girl's head and breasts, but is a wolf below, with a siren's tail. She forces us to have sex in the midst of barking seals and blue sea dogs. We're also afraid of Circe with her vagina dentata, because she's irresistible and able to turn us into docile pigs with men's heads. The bearded women make us laugh, and they generally give us pleasure by using those beards in a special way. Men who are too beautiful seem like monsters to us; we know they feed only on raw meat and honey. We try to avoid their looks, because they would melt us into listless desire. They mate with women who have the whitest skin, but cows' tails and camels' feet. The monster of insomnia inspires us with terror; it has so many eyes and ears that feathers and wings must cover its body so it can fly through the shadows of heaven and earth. However, there are also the ones who speak all the languages of the earth with dreadful facility. They welcome you familiarly in your own language, and thus they trap you easily and eat you quickly, without even starting a fire. They seem to prefer riverbanks, since they are often terribly thirsty. The Harpies have disappeared, and instead of them we watch out for crows that insolently snatch food from the table, right under our noses, like certain very quick ballerina cats. Monsters—even if they speak all languages as we have already heard—are in reality mute. They don't communicate anything. They are creatures of our dreams, and we burst into tears during sleep when they press their weight against our chests. Then the gods of the dawn relieve us, but even at that hour there are snakes that try to wrap themselves around our throats, attempting to drag us to a shore where there is no salvation.

On one wall was written: Celebrate Easter with an egg made of TNT. On another: Jews to the ovens. Together with the ashes of Treblinka, the rain of the impalpable Diossina falls. The time of mutations yields to the time of paralysis, where we all use wheelchairs instead of cars, often with fatal consequences. In the afternoon I was stretched out on the ground so I could feel the breeze that blows from the grass to the leafy branches and back again to the grass—right up to my immobile legs. I felt linked to the air (oxygen enriched with nitrogen!) and the day seemed suspended in a moment of time. Two paws on my back and my face getting soaked. But I'm not afraid—the paws are hands and the tongue belongs to a boy. I sense that he has the erect penis of a small wolf, but not its tail. He's grateful to me for the food and is licking me to ask for more. So I hug him and pet him. I sacrifice another part of the reserve for him. Sperm drips in my groin. He goes to sleep in front of my door, but later when I look for him in the overcast night, I see that he has disappeared. I touch where he was, but don't feel him anymore. He was full, after his little plunder.

Day Thirty-One

Letter No. 27

Small trip to the land of the dead
on the train just out of Catania along the coast
you cross mountains laden with fresh snow
a line of little glaciers or *vendréttes*
the underground station opens toward the summit
the vaults supported by a structure of iron tubes
they come to take us we think they're behind us (She's
 here)
"so much snow in Sicily in the middle of the
 summer!"
but the water's warm and we swim happily
they tell me it's a place where you come to grow old
I stretch out motionless on a rocky spit of land
I look into the transparent depths at the foot of the
 cliff
I think: we'll swim right there or maybe
we'll go in rowboats to warmer areas: toward Turkey
breaking through the defenses of luminous mist
 Turner painted . . .
Now, while telling you this story, as a symbol-maker
I don't know how to explain, so I say only this:
small trip to the land of the dead.

9/30/76

Letter No. 28

if they say: it's a measure
you think: it's a countermeasure
if they say: it's against inflation
you think: it increases inflation
if they say: a stunning blow
you know: this time it must be true
(this letter is as simple
as the game of the three tablets)
even if you know the trick it still works
because Achilles can never catch the tortoise
saying is never the same as doing

10/12/76

Last Christmas was so beautiful. Everyone had poured out into the streets in the cities and towns. On foot, in cars, on bicycles. Clear and cold weather in the North, intermittent gusty rain in the South. But the weather presented no obstacle to the festive ritual of strolling around and meeting people. After months of silence and anxious yapping, the true spirit of this celebration of birth was allowed free play. Cars ran back and forth all night long. The shops were all closed. Be sure you have enough gas in your tank to get there and back, otherwise you'll be on foot or hitch-hiking. Then motors dead forever. They attacked the frozen food warehouses and then cooked it all up in the piazza, sharing with everyone. The comrades provided for all to the utmost of their ability, and then stretched out to sleep in the night's icy cold. In a matter of three or four days the stoppage. History just stopped. But no one thought much about that. The only thing that mattered was what seemed to be gained in the exchange: a renewal of human contacts, the end of the stabbings and shootings seen at every turn just a few hours before; aggression was suspended and provocations were at a level of absolute zero.

First positive result: the disappearance of the clergy. Suddenly they all swarmed away, having ascended to heaven or fallen into hell. The open churches were used for the festival, and even now they're still used as shelters (and I've used them for that myself) or as warehouses, full of bats, sparrows, scorpions, toads, swallows, starlings. The scene of ancient demonic rites no longer practiced, either publicly or privately. Inside grow little stubby plants, dwarf shrubs, bushes, and trees that thrust their branches through windows without panes. On hilltops totems like San Miniato display eyes and bellies that are blind and empty. Looking at them from below, you ask yourself how they inspired such fear, vomiting incense, and gilded processions.

Now the survivors of the festival are living happily as slaves (of whom? everyone, of course!) in order to eat beans. Like the old peasants, they are slaves to the land that starves them, in a new and different way each day. Meat when you can find it: dogs, cats, and mice. But they're very hard to find. If they are found, they're chopped up and thrown into the pot of cooking beans, then fished out. These slaves of everyone know exactly where the gods favor new cultivation—and they are competent hog-raisers. You need to establish yourself where the grass can be cut five times a year, on the edges of the Po's floodplain, and along the riverbanks, as always. The gods, in fact, live in your stomach.

Letter No. 29

sitting in a hall behind windows behind
transparent curtains on the corner of the street
I catch myself in the act of watching how
life outside flows in the form of city traffic
sitting this way I stiffen into immobility
in an almost aulic style I decide to stay there forever
separated from the desire that presses questions
suspending conflict and sinking into rest
in the low light of the dawn this is the hour but
I find the strength to get up because I feel a woolly
flocking of death gather in my lap, a small cat
(when I go out and am forced to walk quickly along
the choice of moving is obligatory but the verb
"to choose" seems appropriate because I had the
    choice
of not getting up again . . .)

10/30/76

Day Thirty-Two

Letter No. 30

I see claws coming out of the walls
others break through the floor
rip up the doors on the armoire
what you call civilization is plunder
industrial or rural
giving and taking means
he only gives who doesn't take

11/14/76

So many blackbirds gleaming in my dream. My dream crossed and recrossed by black motorcycles with chrome sparkling like mirrors. I listen to the whistle of the blackbirds, the roaring sound of motors revving up and slowing down, sounds that overlap one another without drowning each other out. In the end the notes of the blackbirds prevail; they announce the dawn, the first glimmer of light. Just before waking up, I ran into two old men. One asked the other "how are you doing?" and the other replied "it's tough making it from day to day."

I am sure about a thousand signs, especially from dreams. And then they speak about my thin body, my wounds like needle punctures, the diarrhea that alternates with constipation (today a crap like two dark walnuts). All that, together with the happiness of knowing that only a few days remain, maybe two or three. And the feeling of liberation, a way out.

Prey to happiness, I decide to anticipate the end of the story. I want to suspend it now that I'm certain I'm about to disappear. Like a common insect, I notice the hours getting excessively longer until they contain all or almost all of life, to the point where the present is enough in itself—and it stops. Stretched out on my back, I feel my breath raise and lower my chest like celestial movements. The measure of this breathing is self-contained. Power lines cross over me and so many others like me who are still waiting. No one can hold me back or block my passage. I'm beginning to go into that hole overhead, and I'm beginning to come back out of the tunnel. Or I'm beginning to cover myself up, which is the same thing.

Coda. Last movements of my hand. In the half-light of the storeroom, I seem to see the yellow eyes of the boy/wolf. I see them give off a light of cruelty and possession: they want to be the world, they are the world.

This light is the same as the one that deformed my daughter's face for an instant when she said she wanted to eliminate me. I answered by gnashing my teeth.

With this noise the darkness begins, eyelids are lowered and a series of words I no longer understand is pronounced as if they were a roar or a shout that doesn't come out, but goes back down into the throat. That is the way you deny the passage, and the wall of shadow rises instead of lowering. A cat has wisely stretched itself out on my stomach, and it is sleeping. It stays down here with me. Energy and heat disperse slowly. I ask myself where they'll end.

UNIVERSITY PRESS OF NEW ENGLAND publishes books under its own imprint and is the publisher for Brandeis University Press, Brown University Press, University of Connecticut, Darmouth College, Middlebury College Press, University of New Hampshire, University of Rhode Island, Tufts University, University of Vermont, and Wesleyan University Press.

Library of Congress Cataloging-in-Publication Data

Porta, Antonio, 1935–
    [Re del magazzino. English]
    The king of the storeroom / by Antonio Porta ; translated by Lawrence R. Smith.
      p. cm.
    Translation of: Il re del magazzino.
    ISBN 0–8195–5247–X
    I. Title.
  PQ4876.O7R413   1992
853'.914—dc20   91–50819
∞